CONVERGENCE

Visit us at www.boldstrokesbooks.com

By the Author

The Universe Between Us

The Portal Series

Uninvited

Convergence

CONVERGENCE

by

Jane C. Esther

2020

ISBN 13: 978-1-63555-488-5

This Trade Paperback Original Is Published By
Bold Strokes Books, Inc.
P.O. Box 249
Valley Falls, NY 12185

First Edition: June 2020

Credits
Editors: Ashley Tillman and Shelley Thrasher
Production Design: Susan Ramundo
Cover Design By Tammy Seidick

PROLOGUE

Roberto Salazar's lungs burned from the thick, synthetic-rubber fumes choking the air. He was sure someone had started burning tires at the edge of the crowd but couldn't see past the angry mob closing in on him. The blistering sun scorched the pavement, and the asphalt clung to his soles like greedy fingers.

"Give us water or give us death!" the crowd chanted in Portuguese. The heat was brutal, trapping the noise and smell in spirals that assaulted Salazar. He began getting dizzy from the fumes and swallowed the urge to vomit. The crowd pushed against the edge of the concrete barricade. Their faces blurred together into one giant monster with red eyes and angry teeth. Salazar's head spun as the scene before him pitched back and forth. He stepped out, inches from the gray metal door of the watering station, making a show of standing up to the thousands of voices in front of him. Or maybe it was one voice from a thousand people. He wasn't sure anymore. His vision danced across the landscape in pirouettes and leaps.

A father balanced his young son on his shoulders near the front of the group, shouting obscenities that Salazar would never let his own boys hear. The son couldn't have been older than eight, though malnutrition had a stunting effect on children. He looked tired, his eyes pale and sunken. The boy was probably dehydrated or sick because of the water policies, but Salazar couldn't do anything about them. He was a cog in the machine, and he needed that machine to survive. He had direct orders to keep the water station shut until Thursday, when rains were predicted to replenish the reservoirs, if they ever came. The citizens of this São Paulo precinct needed to learn to ration better. There just wasn't enough for everyone. He straightened his military-issue jacket and crossed his arms.

João Oliveira sidled up to him, all five feet two inches of stocky muscle, chest puffed, and heels raised just enough to give him an air of authority he hadn't earned. Salazar had found him annoying in the training academy, but they were as good as friends now.

"Sir, we're getting word of the entire city marching in the streets toward the water stations. We've got about triple this crowd coming toward this one. The commander is sending backup," Oliveira said. His jaw was set, but Salazar could smell the fear radiating from his pores. This was not good.

Salazar widened his stance and tipped his chin a little higher. He spit at the concrete block closest him. This act angered the monster, and the shouting became so loud that he couldn't differentiate one word from another. Not that he cared. His family was back home, safe in one of the government settlements created for loyalists like him. He didn't buy into everything the government was doing, not by a long shot, but he had to ensure his family had access to clean water and enough food. Plus, they paid him a decent salary.

"Salazar, burn in hell!" a protester yelled. A fist-sized rock sailed toward his face and hit the concrete wall behind him with a thud. It left a small dent in the wall and a dusting of gray powder on the ground. He needed to pay more attention if he didn't want to be the next victim.

His radio crackled to life with orders from his commander. "Stand your ground, Watering Station 18. We're sending backup."

He pushed the button and turned toward the receiver on his lapel, ready to copy the orders. Before he could say anything, a low hum began to ring in his ears. Salazar's focus darted around, the mouths of the protestors contorting to form the same angry words they had been shouting. It wasn't them; it was coming from inside him. He shook his head as if that might make the noise go away, but it grew, a horrible grinding, until his ears became instruments of pain. He wanted to scream and cry, a bad look for a soldier, but it didn't matter. His ears felt like they would fall off at any second. He tore at them, growling in frustration. Oliveira stood back with his hand on his gun, a look of disgust on his face.

The noise probed Salazar's brain like tiny hands searching through the mess of pink. The pressure in his head became unbearable, and he reached for his own gun, wanting nothing more than to end his sudden misery. As he lifted the long barrel of the assault rifle to his head, the interminable sound ceased. All Salazar could hear were whispers, words in English like the actors on the American shows his wife watched when their power was on. He looked at Oliveira, but his friend had stepped far away from him, wide-eyed and defensive. When the whispers faded, so did the voices of the mob. No shouting, no screaming, just lips moving in anger.

Salazar gazed into the crowd, at the son on his father's shoulders who probably didn't have enough water in him to spare a single tear, at a trio of young girls who had figured out that anger didn't work and were now begging. Tears ran down their faces and tore at Salazar's stomach, his gut lurching as he felt their sadness. He could almost taste the revulsion his beautiful wife Marta would feel if she saw him guarding this station in the face of such strife. She had a vague idea of what he did, but he'd deliberately left out crucial details to keep her safe. Really, it was his way of shielding her from the hateful person he'd become, willing to let innocent children die because he had orders to deny them water.

When he was a boy, barely eight, the government had begun to impose water restrictions. He'd been sick with diarrhea for days, and his mother had gone out to bolster their dwindling supply of fluids. When she returned, the skin around her eye was beginning to purple, and she walked with a limp. She'd tried to hide it from her son, but he saw the gash on her leg as she'd dressed it in the kitchen. The gallons of brown-tinted water she'd brought back sat idly on the counter like trophies. Salazar had fought his whole life not to be in that position, on that side of the concrete barrier, yet he knew he was as bad as the filth who had beaten a young mother just trying to help her son survive. He was disgusted with himself. All at once, he grasped the machine gun draped across his body, removed the magazine, and threw it to the ground. The noise from the crowd became almost joyful with whoops and hollers.

"What are you doing?" Oliveira asked.

"We've been ordered to abandon post," Salazar said as he walked away.

"By whom?"

"By God."

CHAPTER ONE

The last thing Aerin remembered was the delicious levity of letting go, her body rising, soaring through warm air—the lake that should have glittered in its basin angrily casting her away as it descended beyond its bounds as a roaring tsunami.

She'd left Olivia in the van, trapped and screaming, the kiss still sweet on her lips. She'd straightened her shoulders and walked down to the shore, knowing everything she'd ever wanted was inside that van, pleading with her to turn around. This moment was her destiny, and no matter how much Olivia might miss her, Aerin had to make this sacrifice. Aerin grasped the hands of two people she'd never seen before, and they stepped off the grassy bank into the water. She'd risen then, as if the air beneath her had elevated her on an invisible platform. What followed was a blur.

Now her back throbbed in an unpleasant rhythm that matched her heartbeat, struggling to move diminishing oxygen through her. Aerin couldn't breathe. She grasped the ground around her and felt the knobby fingers of a tree like a blanket underneath. After one more attempt at breathing, she collapsed against the trunk, begging it to help get the water out of her lungs.

She fell onto her back. Warm lips touched hers, and her chest ached to be released. Air in, out again. Pressure in her ribs. Suddenly, the tension broke free, and Aerin coughed, heaving onto her side. She took a few rattling breaths. Olivia was above her, a blur of pale skin and dark hair and stripes. She sounded agitated, her voice strung higher than normal, going on about some kind of bomb. Aerin didn't understand what she meant, though she had a feeling she should know. Olivia's words were coming too fast to make sense. She shut her eyes, wishing Olivia would stop talking. To Aerin's relief, Olivia was silent for a moment. Then she called out a name she recognized from somewhere. Stanton.

Strong arms under her armpits steadied her as she struggled to get to her feet. She leaned into Olivia's warm body, shivering from the dampness that covered the grass, the trees, even Olivia's shirt. It seemed to come from Olivia's eyes, a flood of tears against Aerin's damp hair. No, that couldn't be right. Aerin blinked and saw the hazy lake, peacefully glittering in the sunlight. It felt so familiar, this shore and the dampness. It occurred to her this was the second time she'd been here, the second time she'd been reborn.

"Can you walk to the car?" Olivia asked her. Aerin was far from sure but nodded anyway. "Let's go."

Aerin supported her battered body on unsteady legs, using Olivia as a crutch. Each step tore into a different muscle that screamed for relief. They hobbled toward the lone vehicle, freshly rinsed and shimmering maroon. This is our car, Aerin confirmed to herself. This is where I kissed Olivia, then left her to watch me die. Someone else had been here, too, but she couldn't remember. It was only the two of them now, at any rate. Using her limited energy to probe deeper seemed foolish.

"Here." Olivia opened the back door of the van and pushed aside a few wrappers someone had carelessly thrown on the seat. Aerin vaguely recalled eating some pizza-flavored Combos and poked at the bag as she got in. None left. Too bad. She was ravenous. Her clothing immediately dampened the seat, leaving it uncomfortably squishy. Aerin wished she had a towel, but there wasn't even a blanket. She almost asked Olivia to find her something, but she could tell it seemed more important to Olivia to be safely away from the lake than comfortable. She propped herself against a long side window and stretched her feet across the seat, hugging herself to keep warm. Her sore neck immediately began to twinge at the odd angle, but she didn't bother moving. What was one neck crick in the havoc of the last fifteen minutes?

Sore all over, Aerin turned to watch Olivia hoist herself into the van's driver seat. Olivia blew out a breath and cleared her throat before fumbling with the key, sliding it into the ignition with a shaky hand. Aerin saw her turn the key, but the engine immediately sputtered out.

"I swear I saw Stanton," Olivia said. She stared at Aerin in the rearview mirror. Her eyes were strangely disembodied in the reflection. Stanton. The name sounded familiar, but she couldn't place it. "Shit. And Murray's gone. He's just gone, fucking disappeared. What the fuck?" Olivia hit the steering wheel with the heels of her hands, and Aerin jumped. Calm down, she thought. Olivia sighed.

Murray. That was who they came with. Now that she remembered, Aerin could feel his presence in the van like the old man had never followed her outside and into destruction. She pictured him in the backseat rolling his eyes and delivering scathing commentary. Aerin smiled at his memory. She'd miss him. A sob drew her attention, and she craned her neck to see Olivia leaning into the steering wheel. It was the most mournful sound Aerin had ever heard. She reached to touch what she could reach of Olivia's hair through the headrest. As soon as she did, as if those had been the extent of Olivia's emotions, she sniffled and turned the key again. The waterlogged engine sputtered for a few seconds longer but still wouldn't start. A few tries later, it came to life.

"All the other cars, all the people," Olivia said. Aerin should know what Olivia meant, but she couldn't think of what it was, so she closed her eyes and gave in to exhaustion.

Sometime later, roused by the van ceasing its lulling motion, Aerin woke with a start. They had stopped in front of a nondescript motel, the kind you'd find on true-crime TV where murderers stayed before and after they killed. Dirty white chairs stood watch outside the rooms next to rusty coffee cans for cigarettes. She cringed at the suggestion of smoking. She didn't need reminders of her ex-husband Josh right now.

Her head was clearer after the nap, though her chest was still sore, and a spot in her lower rib cage stabbed with each breath. As predicted, her neck had cramped where it bent against the window. She rubbed it and peered out at the mostly empty motor-lodge parking lot. This was a pull-in place—stay for a couple of hours, then get the hell out. She hoped Olivia wasn't getting them a room here.

A small brown bird landed on the hood of the car and hopped to the windshield, where it looked inside, cocked its tiny head, and made a chittering sound.

"Hi, little fellow," she said in a sing-song voice.

The bird jumped onto the windshield wiper with small, quick movements, pooped on the glass, and flew away. Aerin groaned.

As she waited for Olivia to come out, she wondered if anything that happened today had been real. Maybe her entire life since she'd first set foot in those waters had all been one long nightmare. The thought comforted her even as she sensed its absurdity. Wasn't it as unbelievable to think she'd actually lived through it? As she was constructing scenarios for how she might wake herself up, Olivia emerged from around the corner of the building. Aerin's stomach dropped when she saw her expression. Olivia's brow was knitted so tightly Aerin thought she might combust at any second.

Olivia opened the van's side door with a heave, exposing Aerin to the outside air. It was suddenly harder to imagine she was dreaming. Olivia must have changed at some point. She'd exchanged the striped shirt that had been in Murray's drawings for one of her solid tees, and her pants looked dry. It was her worry that was uncharacteristic. She didn't look like herself, though Aerin couldn't remember Olivia ever looking any other way.

"We're staying here for a couple of days. I just want to make sure we're okay to get back home."

"Where are we?" Aerin asked.

"Wish I could remember what the sign said. Some tiny town about forty-five minutes from Geneva. South, I think. You were out like a light the entire drive." She tried to smile, but her expression came across as a worried grimace.

Aerin tried to sit up and gasped in pain. This must be the "okay to get back home" bit Olivia was talking about. She wasn't fit to travel in any way other than lying in the backseat of a van. As Olivia helped her out, another memory returned. They'd saved people, a lot of them. And then, as if a haze had suddenly evaporated in the fresh air, she remembered everything. It came back like a speeding train through her mind, loud and out of control. Could it be true? Had she caused an explosion that sent a beacon to another universe? Had the Rhunans been summoned to Earth? She stumbled over her feet as they walked toward the building, shocked that she'd taken part in something so seismic and preposterous at the same time.

"You okay?" Olivia asked.

Aerin lied. "Uh-huh."

The room was a lot nicer than she'd expected, though it still fit low-budget stereotypes. Dark-blue drapes outlined the two parking-lot-facing windows and contrasted nicely with the minimalist white palette of the rest of the room. She shivered as she neared the air conditioner, set to 65 on this warm day. Olivia must have seen her staring at the buttons for too long, because she came over and shut it off. Better, Aerin thought. Best would be to get into some dry clothes. A sweatshirt and sweatpants would be ideal, though she was positive she hadn't brought any. Olivia set their bags in the bathroom, then collapsed onto the end of the bed with her head in her hands. With modesty at the bottom of her list of cares, Aerin stripped off her clothes and climbed under the covers. Olivia didn't even notice, a testament to how upset she must be. Prior to today, Aerin knew Olivia would have been tempted to climb in after her.

Aerin closed her eyes and got comfortable. The stiff sheets and detergent smell jogged something else in her mind. "We were in a hotel before we came here. Murray was with us."

"Yeah," Olivia said after a while. She sniffled. "I guess he drowned."

Aerin thought for a moment about Murray. What she saw in her mind soothed her. "No," Aerin said.

"What?" Olivia whipped around.

She felt a smile creep across her face. "He's in a better place."

"Dead is a better place?"

"No. You don't understand."

"And you do?"

Aerin propped herself up on her elbows. A lot of thoughts were coming to her now in pieces, floating steadily back into her head from the river of her memory. A shiver ran down her spine, and she remembered Murray turning toward her just as the waterspout was about to crash down. He'd smiled and nodded. "Take it from here, kid."

"I do," Aerin said.

CHAPTER TWO

S tanton sat in a bar, one of his old haunts, the kind of place where the right gossip got you free booze, and nobody cared where you were from. The bartender wiped the shiny oak counter with a sooty cloth that only provided the illusion of cleanliness. "Is there anything else I can get you, Mr…?"

"Owens. Robert Owens. And no, thank you." Stanton gulped down half his large mug of beer. Awful stuff, but this wasn't exactly the century when microbreweries would pop up in every abandoned warehouse. He'd had no choice but to go back as far as possible—two hundred years—to gather the people whose long-forgotten existences would usher in a new beginning for the planet and beyond. He was in the same town where he became part Rhunan, that same lake nearby without scores of luxury mansions built upon its banks, dotting the horizon like an elite border garden.

A dozen half-drowned men and women sputtered and coughed on each other at a table in the corner. It had cost Stanton a large sum of energy to manipulate time with so many witnesses to convince, but he didn't have a choice. He needed a certain number of people to open the portal, and it was much easier to take them from a time when public records weren't too accurate. Plus, he had the bonus of nobody believing the fantastical stories from the disreputable people he'd chosen. Enormous waterspout? Drinking too much or hallucinating from illness.

The room was dark at the edges and smelled like fire and roasting meat. Gas lanterns lit the bar. Small candles adorned the tables, occupied mostly by men in various stages of drunkenness.

Stanton checked to make sure none of the people in his group
had inhaled too much water and turned back to the bartender.
"Anything strange happen here recently, last day or so?"

The bartender stopped wiping and eyed Stanton. "Why, you
know something?"

Stanton knew the bartender was simply looking for gossip he
could trade away, but he had to be careful. "Just heard some stories."
He took another swig of his beer. Behind him, the coughing faded,
and a stream of whispers passed amongst his group. There was too
much noise in the room to tell if the hushed sounds were in his
head, out loud, or both.

"You'll have to talk to the sheriff. He's trying to find those
young men who disappeared. Heard they were farmhands up at the
Bartlett property, and two days ago, they just up and left."

"Hm. Strange. Hadn't heard about that, but I did hear about
some disreputable ladies who've been kidnapped." Stanton smiled
to himself. In the shadows cast by the lanterns, the bartender
couldn't make out his expression. Stanton would know. All of this
had already happened before.

The man sighed and tucked the rag into his tweed pants.
"Those girls from that whorehouse over in Newark? They go
missing all the time, and nobody gives a horse's bit about them.
Same story every week."

Stanton shuddered despite himself, even though he'd heard
this before. This was the callousness he'd lived with and probably
possessed before he stepped into that lake and his life had changed
forever. If he had his way, and he would sometime around the mid-
twenty-first century, he'd make the entire world wake up to their
corrupt ways.

Stanton skidded the wobbly oak barstool away from the
counter and thanked the bartender. He caught a few dirty looks as
he weaved through the crowd to the corner table. He was currently
an outsider in this town, though he'd end up spending so much of
his life here that their disregard was laughable.

He nodded to the thoroughly confused group of men and
women who had just been thrown two centuries ahead, pretended

to drive twenty-first century gargantuan metal vehicles and worn strange, futuristic clothes, at least in their minds. Then he closed his eyes and began to hum, thankful he could advance past the time when the explosion had finally come to pass.

When he opened them, he found he had miscalculated. He'd meant to go back to Dr. Perralta's lab, where he was working on coding one of her computer simulation programs. Instead, he was back at the lake moments after the explosion, according to Aerin and Olivia. 2019. Really, it was sometime between those two points, a random moment he'd picked where nobody would be around to pay attention, closer to the lifetimes of his helpers. The grass still sparkled with lake water, which would fade at any moment as the illusion dissolved for Olivia and Aerin. They were already beginning to see their present, and Stanton hadn't intended to be in it. He kept the illusion going for longer, long enough that the women wouldn't suspect anything.

Olivia was running toward Aerin, who leaned against a tree, unconscious. He watched as Olivia resuscitated her, then muttered hysterically about the explosion. As she clamored for Aerin's full attention, Stanton realized he was visible behind a tree. She glanced in his direction and caught him there. She seemed to stare at him forever. Stanton chuckled at what must be going through her mind. If she only realized the half of it. He wasn't worried at his misstep, though. He held her gaze for a moment before disappearing behind the tree. Whether she saw him didn't matter. The message had been sent, and the primary messenger was propped against a tree, alive. Those were his two objectives.

He moved the three of them out of the time loop at the same time he converged with his body in Dr. Perralta's lab. His hands had never stopped typing, though he must have been unresponsive. Stanton wasn't entirely sure how he would look to an outsider, but he needn't have worried. What was done was done. He leaned back in the chair and smiled ominously. He'd almost completed his mission.

CHAPTER THREE

The local police station was almost empty the morning after the explosion. It was just by chance that Olivia had driven past it in search of a good breakfast. Walsh, the officer taking Olivia's statement, huffed and leaned from one foot to the other. His uniform shirt ballooned toward the bottom, covering a beer belly he'd surely perfected with decades of commitment.

"You're sure?" Olivia asked.

"I'm sure."

"Nothing?"

"Ma'am, I'm not sure what you think you saw, but there's no way it could have been an explosion of that size. I guarantee you everyone from here to the White House would be aware of something like that. Are you positive you haven't taken any drugs recently?" Officer Walsh looked at his watch and sipped a cup of coffee. Olivia could tell he was eager to get the crazy woman out of there and move on with his day.

Olivia took a deep breath. Did she look like she'd just taken a bunch of hallucinogens? Possibly. She'd put on new clothes but hadn't really done anything to her hair. She needed about fifty showers and a week of sleep, and to stop talking to this energy sap immediately. She wished she was already back at the hotel with breakfast to feed a sleeping Aerin, warm and very much alive under the covers. Only this morning had she noticed that Aerin was at least partly nude under there. It had to be the first time she'd unknowingly slept in the same bed as a sexy, naked woman. She blushed and cleared her throat.

"So, just to clarify there was no strange activity in Geneva yesterday?"

"Ms. Ando, I just texted the chief over there, and she hasn't had any reports of any activity of any sort. She said the park looked the same as it always does. It was just a normal day."

Like hell it was. "Okay, well, thank you. I guess I'll chalk it up to an active imagination."

The officer shook her hand and gestured toward the exit. Olivia walked numbly through the main doors of the police station and to the van. As she opened the front door, a trickle of water fell from the gasket. As far as she knew, it hadn't rained last night. She might be going crazy, but she wasn't making this up.

If the police wouldn't help her, she'd have to figure it out for herself. Usually she enjoyed research and was even good at it, but right now, the thought of doing anything other than taking a mid-morning nap exhausted her. She leaned the seat back, took out her phone, and checked Twitter for any reports of weird stuff happening in Geneva. A search for #Geneva pulled up only a notice about a bluegrass festival that would take place there next weekend. How could nobody else have seen? And where the fuck had Stanton come from? She was sure it had been him darting behind a tree. His bald head and glasses, along with the slightly odd look in his eyes, were unmistakable. Stanton, Aerin, and Olivia. The only three survivors of an event that seemed not to have taken place.

She called Jody. If nobody else knew anything, at least Jody, her best friend and colleague, could confirm that Stanton was out of town for the weekend. She almost hung up the phone immediately after remembering the time difference, but Jody usually turned her phone off at night. Besides, even though it was the weekend, Jody should be up by now. She reached Jody's voice mail and left a message.

"Hey, can you do me a favor and find out if Stanton is in New York for some reason? I thought I saw him and just wanted to know if it was him or his doppelgänger." She chuckled a little to make her question sound less dire. "Okay, talk to you later."

Olivia leaned back against the headrest and closed her eyes. Stanton and Aerin. There were only two people she could talk to about this, and one of them was conveniently a short drive away.

CHAPTER FOUR

A erin stirred as Olivia's arm slipped around her middle. She ran her fingers along the ropey muscles, and Olivia let out a harsh breath. Aerin leaned back into her as if their closeness would erase the last decade and a half. She needed to be against Olivia, with and in her. Aerin felt Olivia's lips graze the nape of her neck, and she pulled the hand up to her breast, praying Olivia would recognize how much she couldn't wait to feel those fingers again.

She moaned as the pressure sent chills of pleasure through her body. "Mmm, Olivia."

"Aerin?"

"Yes," she whispered breathlessly.

"Wake up."

"Hm?" Aerin became conscious of a hand on her boob. When she realized it was her own, she rolled over to face Olivia and opened her eyes a smidge. Olivia was standing over the bed, arms crossed, a biting smile on her face.

"Having a little dream there?"

"No." Aerin made sure her hands were out in the open, where Olivia could see them.

"Hm. Don't know whether to believe you."

Aerin's cheeks burned. "You should believe me. I was just, uh, practicing. For a play I'm writing."

"About someone named Olivia?"

"If you must know, yes."

"Hm."

Real or imagined, Aerin was on fire. Olivia smirked and sat on the bed, raising her hand to reach toward her. Her breath hitched, unsure for a moment of Olivia's intentions. When Olivia merely squeezed her hand, Aerin shuddered. The electricity of Olivia's desire burned through her skin. It was a sharper current than when Olivia had been waffling about whether the two of them could or should get back together. She was used to that. No, this was something new, something raw. For the first time since they were teens, Olivia seemed to want what Aerin did, was almost ready to go all in.

Aerin didn't want to make the first move. She'd already made that mistake, albeit accidentally, in the hospital storeroom. The memory of their misunderstanding sobered her. She sat up in bed and grabbed for a T-shirt on the floor. Olivia's dark eyes were on her the whole time.

"Stop staring," she said. She hoped Olivia wouldn't listen to her.

"You don't need help, do you?" Olivia didn't look like she was in any hurry to move.

Aerin rolled her eyes and smacked Olivia with the balled-up shirt.

"Maybe we should talk about what happened in the van. When you kissed me."

So kissing was on Olivia's mind. The details of the van kiss were hazy. She remembered telling Olivia she'd never stopped loving her, and then she'd leaned in for the most electric, explosive kiss she'd ever experienced. Regret, promise, and eternal devotion painted her tongue. The kiss had been good-bye. Aerin hadn't expected to make it through the bomb. At Murray's apartment, she hadn't found a drawing beyond the picture of them at the lake. She'd assumed that after that moment, it was over for her. Now that she examined the aftermath, it was clear that Murray hadn't seen anything beyond that moment because he wasn't alive anymore. For him, nothing beyond existed.

"Earth to Aerin."

Aerin snapped back to attention. She ignored the ache of grief in her chest. "Right, the kiss. I'm up for doing it again whenever you're ready."

Olivia shifted carefully, scrunching her brow as she tried to find words. "I just want to make sure you're you again. Are you?"

What a strange question. I've always been me, Aerin thought. "Something happened when the bomb went off. I feel different now."

"So it's gone?"

Aerin had two choices. Tell Olivia the truth, that she didn't think two independent entities existed inside her anymore, but couldn't pinpoint the reason, or tell her what she wanted to hear.

"I think so. I'm not hungry anymore, not like I was. That's a good sign that it's gone." Aerin was pleased with her answer, a safe, vague explanation. She did feel slightly more stable than she had before, when crazy, racing thoughts were bombarding her all the time. Plus, she realized, she'd just had a dream about something other than an underwater mass drowning.

Olivia's eyes darkened and she moved infinitesimally closer, her gaze sliding deftly from Aerin's mouth back to her eyes. Aerin's cheeks burned, and her stomach clenched in anticipation. This was the moment. She wanted this so badly it hurt. As Olivia's lips were about to touch hers, the warmth of her breath dancing across Aerin's skin, someone knocked on the door.

Olivia pulled back quickly, as if she'd been caught doing something wrong. Come back, Aerin thought. Olivia hesitated, looking between Aerin and the door, then got up to answer.

"Your car the maroon van?" asked an older man who was just out of Aerin's line of sight.

"Uh, yeah. How can I help you?"

"Lights are going on and off. Might want to see if some alarm's tripped on it."

Olivia turned to Aerin and shrugged. "Okay. We'll take a look." She closed the door and leaned against it, her face still flushed from their almost-kiss, chest heaving.

Aerin didn't know how someone could look so appealing in a roadside motel in the middle of nowhere. This was supposed to be a murder motel, not the place where she'd finally get to kiss Olivia again. She propped herself up on one elbow. "You going to check it out?"

Olivia stared at her for a moment before answering. "Yeah."

Aerin watched her go, cursing the man who had interrupted. She flopped onto her back and blew out a breath. Her nerves were electric. Just the thought of Olivia's lips on hers again was so tantalizing, she was afraid to touch her own skin for fear of implosion.

When Olivia returned a couple minutes later, she sat in the rolling desk chair and barely looked at the bed. Aerin tried to read her mind, but something had changed, and she couldn't seem to extend her reach to the other side of the small room. Maybe the alien was gone after all. Olivia took her phone out of her pocket and tapped the screen.

"Hm." She pulled her knees to her chest and frowned.

"What's up?"

"Oh, nothing. Just a message from Jody." Olivia looked at her as if suddenly remembering what they'd been doing before the knock. Her cheeks flushed, but she didn't move.

"Want to get some brunch?" Aerin asked. She was getting hungry, though she hesitated to mention it for fear that Olivia would think the alien was still there. As predicted, Olivia studied her for a moment, a hint of suspicion in her eyes.

"Actually, I'm hungry, too. Why don't you look through this big binder and see if you can find a menu that'll work." She picked up a weathered white binder from the desk and tossed it onto the bed. "I'm going to shower."

Olivia took such a long time in the bathroom that Aerin wondered whether getting clean was all she was doing. The room began to feel like a jungle, sticky and humid, with a cloying odor. She'd lined up an entire week's worth of meals by the time Olivia emerged glistening with a freshly showered sheen, wrapped in a towel.

"Sorry for being so long."

"You do what you need to do," Aerin said under her breath. Olivia either didn't hear or didn't acknowledge the comment, and Aerin took it as confirmation that Olivia had put the shower head to good use. She looked intently at the menu she'd just pulled out to distract herself from Olivia's closeness. "How's this? Could be awful, but looks good on paper. It's not too far from here."

She handed Olivia the menu for a family restaurant and waited for her to read it. The smell of cheap hotel soap filled her nostrils. Normally, Aerin wouldn't be so attracted to the slightly off-putting perfume of cheap hotel shampoo, but damned if she wasn't leaning closer to get a better whiff from Olivia.

"Did you just smell me?" The hint of a smile curled at the corner of Olivia's lips.

Caught. "Yeah. Is that a problem?"

"Maybe. I don't know."

"Well, you let me know if you figure it out."

"I will."

Aerin wasn't certain they were talking about the sniffing anymore. Olivia bit her lip in a way that made Aerin glad she hadn't tried to kiss her again. The proof was in the hesitation. Olivia wasn't 100 percent sure about rekindling their old flame. Aerin understood, though she wished it were easier. Why couldn't they just act on their very obvious feelings for each other? What more could she do to prove she wanted to be with Olivia?

"This is fine with me," Olivia said.

Her voice pulled Aerin from her thoughts. "Huh?" Olivia gave her a look. "Right. Food."

"I'll get dressed."

Too bad, Aerin thought, but she said nothing. Instead, she sniffed her armpits and brazenly walked almost naked to the bathroom to shower. She tried not to think about the hot woman changing in the other room. Her sex drive was out of control today, which would have been great if she had been with a willing participant. If she had any extra money at all, she'd suggest they rent separate rooms just so she could get a bit of relief. This was insane.

When she emerged from the bathroom, Olivia had changed into some black athletic pants and a T-shirt. No bra. Aerin tried not to think about whether that detail was purposeful. Olivia wasn't that cruel, was she? After all, she didn't absolutely need a bra. Aerin had the opposite problem, garnering rude stares from anyone who saw her in public without one.

"Interested in something?" Olivia asked, hands on her hips.

"Sorry?"

"You're looking at my chest like it's made of candy."

"It's not?"

Olivia playfully smacked her on the arm. "Hey. Stop objectifying me."

"Stop being so damn hot." Aerin pursed her lips so that nothing else like that would slip out of them.

"On that note, let's go. And no, I'm not trying to command your attention by not wearing a bra. I just didn't feel like it."

"I wasn't even wondering that," Aerin lied.

"I'm sure you weren't."

The restaurant Aerin had chosen was a few towns over and turned out to host a mouthwatering breakfast buffet every morning from eight to noon. Folks who looked like part of the usual crowd ambled in and out, greeting the waitstaff by name and asking how so-and-so was doing. The favorite pieces of attire in this area seemed to be adorned with the Buffalo Bills' logo. Aerin and Olivia ate until they were stuffed, leaning gingerly against opposite sides of the booth.

Olivia held her stomach. "I'll definitely need to walk this off."

"Same. I feel like I've angered the stomach gods. They might not let me get up for a few more minutes," Aerin said. She really had to pee, but she also really had to digest. That last French-toast stick wasn't doing her any favors.

"Well, when we're ready to move again, you up for doing something touristy? I saw a brochure rack out front. Want me to grab some?"

"Yeah." Aerin groaned. "Oof." The fullness wasn't helping her bruises from yesterday, although they were much improved.

She didn't hurt every time she breathed any more, just a subtle ache once in a while.

Aerin picked at the remaining home fries on her plate until Olivia returned. Apparently, by "some" brochures, she'd meant all of them. They shuffled through the thirty-odd advertisements for Finger Lakes activities until Aerin came across a picture of a waterfall.

"This looks pretty. Let's go here." She slid the brochure to Olivia, who studied it.

"Looks awesome. You sure you want to be around falling water, though?"

Aerin deflated. "Hadn't thought about that."

"I'll be honest. I don't know if I can handle it."

"How about this bird sanctuary instead?" Aerin handed her another brochure, this time for a National Wildlife Refuge. It also seemed to contain water, though it was the kind that collected in ponds and slow-moving rivers and didn't fall from terrifying heights.

"You got it," Olivia said easily. They looked at each other and smiled. If this was a date, it would be so hard for Aerin not to make the first move.

CHAPTER FIVE

"You didn't believe me when I told you it was bird poop."
Olivia laughed at Aerin's sourness. "Come on. It'll wash right off in the shower."

She used the key, an actual brass implement that was either a throwback or had never really gone out of style here, to open the door to their room. Aerin pushed around her to get out of the way of additional birds that might have thoughts about where to drop their excrement.

"This is just so categorically disgusting."

"The bird itself was adorable. Even you thought so."

Aerin rubbed her hands over her face in chagrin. "Yeah, before it shit on my head."

"Technically, it's the same bird before and after, so same cuteness level."

Aerin shot daggers with her eyes. "If you do not go into the bathroom and turn on that shower for me right now, I will open your suitcase and rub my hair on everything in there."

"Whoa, whoa, okay, princess. I'm going." Still giggling, Olivia trotted over to the bathroom and winked before she went in.

"Damn birds," Aerin said.

"I heard that. Mr. Piddles is a bird, don't you forget."

"Mr. Piddles did not shit in my hair."

"Yet. Bound to happen."

"Can't wait," she said.

Aerin washed her hair three times to get the filth out and conditioned it for the full five minutes the tiny bottle recommended. When she tried to put a brush through it, though, well, that wouldn't happen.

"Olivia, can you come here for a second?"

"Yeah?" Olivia opened the door a few inches and poked her head in.

Aerin quickly covered up with the towel at her feet. "Whoa. Holy crap. I didn't say come in. I just meant come to the door."

"You said come here," Olivia said.

"Yes, come to the door so I can talk to you."

"How was I supposed to know?" Olivia hadn't moved from her vantage point and looked like she was content to enjoy the view.

Aerin rolled her eyes. "I need you to do me a favor and get me some leave-in conditioner. Do you see my hair?"

"Yeah. Looks like the bird that pooped on your head also made a nest there."

"Thanks, asshole."

"No problem. So do you have any details about this leave-in conditioner you want, or should I just grab whatever I see first?"

Aerin thought for a moment. Was it the blue or green bottle that had worked the best last time? "Just get me whatever."

"Okay."

"You can stop staring at me now."

Olivia nodded like she was weighing that option, then disappeared. The door to their room opened and shut.

"Christ," Aerin said. Now she was hot and bothered, but too annoyed with her hair to do anything about it.

Olivia returned with the blue and green bottles of conditioner Aerin had been thinking about. Maybe her powers hadn't changed as much as she thought. Aerin used a little of both to soothe her ratty mane. After a late-evening snack of granola bars Olivia had also picked up, they settled into bed to watch TV.

The later it got, the more awkward things became between them. Olivia was at one edge of the bed and Aerin at the other, as if distance could soothe the tension they'd been able to avoid most of the day through activity. Had they kissed that morning, it might have broken the electric current. Instead, Aerin wondered what would happen when it was time to sleep. Would they sleep back-to-back? Head-to-toe? Would she be able to stop herself from ghosting Olivia's skin with her fingertips during the night?

Finally, the only shows on were infomercials, and though Olivia pretended to be interested, Aerin definitely wasn't.

"I'm going to sleep," she said. She burrowed under the covers as far to the edge as she could, wrapping herself tightly in the sheet. Olivia would have to stick with the comforter.

A few moments later, Olivia turned off the TV and settled into bed. A few minutes after that, she rolled onto her other side. Then back. Aerin marked these movements because she couldn't sleep either. Even though she faced the other way, she could tell Olivia was facing her back. Finally, she couldn't stand it any longer and turned around.

Olivia's eyes were wide open, filled with fear and longing, visible from the streetlights outside that peeked around the blackout curtains. How could someone simply looking at her be so erotic? Aerin gulped hard and reached to touch Olivia's hand on the pillow between them. The loud air conditioner seemed to fade into oblivion, the sound replaced by Olivia's breathing, shallow and rapid with anticipation. Slowly, Aerin ran her fingers up Olivia's arm to her shoulder. Her own heartbeat thudded in her ears.

Olivia tentatively touched Aerin's cheek, sending chills radiating in all directions from Aerin's spine. She couldn't believe how much she wanted this moment to last forever, and how much she wanted to move to the next. The light from outside painted an orange stripe across Olivia's skin as she slid nearer. The heat from their bodies mingled between them, a sweaty mess of pulsating energy. She pulled Olivia closer, savoring the moment of greatest potential, that moment right before the birth of something new. Their lips almost touched, nanometers between them, but Aerin would wait until Olivia kissed her. She would wait, she told herself again and again as the moment stretched to eternity. She would hold out as long as it took, on fire, chest pounding like a timpani.

Olivia's resolve snapped, and she pressed her warm lips against Aerin's, turning her head slightly into the pillow to get the perfect angle. And what an angle it was. Aerin moaned as their tongues met, and she intertwined their legs, unable to get as close to Olivia as she wanted. With clothes on, this would have to do.

"I can't believe you still turn me on this much," Olivia said after they broke apart. The sheets were damp, and Aerin's lips were sore. Not that she was complaining.

"How much exactly?"

"I'm out of my fucking mind," Olivia whispered as she rolled on top.

CHAPTER SIX

Olivia bought airplane tickets for the trip home. She and Aerin were more than a little exhausted from the night before and not at all fit to drive. It had been a full week since they'd been in Indiana, and as much as she wanted the extra vacation time with Aerin, Olivia had some work responsibilities to get back to. Besides, if they were going to do nothing but what they'd done last night, they deserved a real bed in a real bedroom.

Aerin's best friend Zoe picked them up from the airport in her red Magnum. Almost immediately she began peppering them with questions about the trip. After all, she hadn't even realized Aerin was gone. Olivia could tell Zoe suspected something had shifted between them. She kept stealing glances at Aerin and then in the rearview mirror at Olivia, who sat silently for most of the ride. She was more content to replay scenes from last night than engage in meaningless conversation. Luckily, Aerin indulged Zoe with a barrage of half-truths about where they'd gone and who they'd seen.

They reached Olivia's house, not far from the Indianapolis airport, too quickly. Stepping out of the car meant that Zoe would start asking Aerin for the juicy details. It also meant that Aerin would go home to Tireville, a whole hour away, and Olivia would have to wait to kiss her again. Her inability to keep her hands off Aerin since last night surprised her. Luckily, they'd been separated by the seating arrangement in the car. Zoe would get quite an earful.

The car pulled to a stop in Olivia's driveway. "Thanks for the ride, Zoe." Olivia squeezed Zoe's shoulder from the back seat and shuffled out of the car. "Aerin, I'll see you tomorrow?" Aerin blew her a kiss from the passenger's side that left her light-headed. An air kiss was the best she'd get tonight. Olivia blushed all the way to her dark front door. Before she had time to take out her keys, Zoe pulled out of her driveway, and the headlights drifted away from her until the only light came from the one working streetlight a few houses over. She was alone.

Olivia leaned against the door frame for a moment before sitting on her top step. The flight had drained her energy, the little that remained. The past week felt like a never-ending year, and Olivia hadn't had so many things happen to her in the past five. Getting back together with Aerin, stopping a bomb from creating a tidal wave that would have wiped out a small city, watching a whole group of people march to their deaths—it was too much. Olivia put her head in her hands and began to cry.

After she'd exhausted her reserves and the droning of crickets and cicadas became too much, she finally went inside. Mr. Piddles, her African grey parrot, squawked and shrieked for a good ten minutes after she opened the door to his room. "I've only been gone for a week, buddy. You love your Aunt Jody."

"I missed you. I missed you," he said again and again. She hadn't left him for more than a few days in her whole life, poor thing. "Why did you leave me?"

Olivia kissed him on the beak while she stroked his silky feathers. "I'm sorry. I missed you, too. I had to help save people. It was for a good cause, I promise."

Jody had kept the house in such good shape for the week that Olivia felt like she was standing in some kind of model home. Even through the lens of her own slightly compulsive cleaning streak, this was clean with a capital C. She made a note to buy Jody her favorite German chocolate cake the next time she saw her.

Mr. Piddles hopped around the living room while Olivia reclined on the couch. She had six new episodes of *Sunrise Lane* on her DVR, and she put them on for background noise. Mr. Piddles bounced about a little before settling on her leg. He'd probably poop on the couch, but she'd deal with that later. She was too exhausted to care.

She woke up in the early morning hours to an infomercial for a chicken rotisserie. The sight of a chicken carcass dripping with juices turned her stomach, and she grasped blindly for the remote. She couldn't turn it off soon enough. Without the light from the TV, she blinked against the darkness. She whispered for Mr. Piddles, but he'd left. He was probably back in his room sleeping on his perch. Unfortunately, she had been right about the poop. She felt it against her toes as she pivoted to a sitting position. So much for a model home. She stepped delicately to the bathroom, balancing on one and a half feet.

Now that she was awake, Olivia's stomach rumbled. She hadn't eaten since the airport, and she'd only had a salad then. A quick perusal of her fridge was as disappointing as she'd assumed. A tub of yogurt that might have gone bad, ketchup, mustard, and pickles. The fridge of a bachelor. She closed the door and noticed a note on her counter.

Lasagna in freezer. Eat more. Love, Jody

God, she loved that woman. Olivia microwaved and ate the culinary masterpiece until she was uncomfortably full, satisfying her hunger and temporarily stifling the part of her that yearned for answers about the past couple of months. Nighttime brought too many thoughts into focus, and she couldn't possibly process them all. Too stuffed to go back to sleep, she made a cup of tea and settled back on the clean side of the couch to work through them.

In hindsight, the past week seemed more like an out-of-body experience than something she'd witnessed in person. No, she hadn't just witnessed it; she'd taken part in all of it. She hadn't been herself. She'd stolen hospital equipment, for fuck's sake. What had she been thinking? Had she been thinking? Not at first. Who knew how much Aerin had been thinking for her.

Maybe she was in her right mind, though, which made her complicit in the insanity. And she had to face the facts. Aerin had predicted there would be an explosion, and that had turned out to be true, at least according to her own account. Maybe the thing in Aerin's head was a real alien. The thing that had been in her head, Olivia thought. Past tense. It was gone now. Aerin was back to normal. She'd seen it in the sudden shift to calm, in Aerin's happiness that wasn't wrapped up in mania.

The darkness outside was just beginning to lift, and a couple of loud blue jays outside the living-room window started to screech. Olivia yawned, desperate to go back to sleep, but not hopeful it would happen. She showered. Maybe that might lull her back into slumber as the rest of the world was just waking. She stayed under the spray longer than she'd intended, letting the water pelt her shoulders with increasing heat until she couldn't stand it any longer. A shower to wash away her past and all the emotional grime that came with it.

Olivia was still wide awake as the sky became ringed with the first bursts of light. She tried reading the news on her phone, but it was too depressing. She tried playing a dull phone game, but she ran out of lives. Finally, she opened her email to go through the latest batch and ended up conducting a major clean-out. The things the brain was willing to focus on in the early hours astounded her.

As she scrolled past departmental-meeting messages, university-wide announcements, and professional-organization spam, she found the email with Stanton's sound recording. That first recording that had sent Aerin spiraling into painful oblivion and Olivia flying through space until she almost crashed into a marigold ocean. Her thumb hovered over the screen as she weighed the possibility she'd made it all up. She'd been dreaming, surely, and even if she hadn't been, the music had served its purpose. It wouldn't have anything new to show her, would it?

"Why the hell not?" She opened the file, laid back against the pillow, and closed her eyes. The unpleasant saxophone melody was familiar to her now. She hummed along and took a deep breath that forced the tension to drain from her body. The music had done its magic only when she'd been on the verge of sleep. Her mind was most open then, vulnerable, and attempting to recreate that state wouldn't be easy.

She gave it her all for some time, pretending she was floating in an ocean, firmly grounded, even soaring through the air, but the music looped on and on in the background. She was still in her bed, in her room, on Earth. With a sigh, she rolled onto her side and buried her cheek in the soft pillow. She yawned and blinked heavily a few times against the rising light, and then she was asleep.

Olivia opened her front door and stepped out into the brilliantly lit morning. The air was fragrant with late-summer greenery, and she filled her lungs with its sweetness. The beauty of the day temporarily distracted her from the fact that she had no clue where the hell she was. To her left, she expected to see the vast cornfield that was part of the Tillman farm. Instead, a young forest grew there, tree branches reaching out toward each other and into the sky. In the other direction, in place of her neighbors' boring, uniform houses, sprawled ruins overgrown with vines and shrubs. Too much change for one morning, Olivia thought, so she turned to go back inside, but the house was gone, and she stood on steps that led to nowhere.

The stairs were made of a strange material, some kind of gray memory foam. She shifted her weight from foot to foot, feeling their heft beneath her. Her feet sank into the springy softness the perfect amount. Somehow, the material propelled her down to the bottom, into something that looked like grass from above but, upon closer inspection, had tendrils that looped back into the ground. Delighted, Olivia bent to touch it. A strand reached out toward her finger and sprang back at the contact.

Warmth spread through her neck and down her arms. The sun was brighter than she was used to, but not as strong. A pleasant breeze carried an earthy smell through the air, and Olivia shivered as the wind tickled her skin. Nobody was around, no cars or basketball hoops, American flags or clay pots of geraniums. The street was shiny, and she stepped onto it. She immediately slipped and fell against its unforgiving hardness. It was made of slick metal or heavy plastic, maybe a rock like obsidian. Her wrist was straining away from the surface, and she was wearing a metal watch. Huh. Definitely a strong magnet. Where the hell was she?

The street stretched far in either direction, too far for her to see what was at the end. On one side, the forest seemed to devour the road, but on the other, it might have gone on for miles. She carefully walked down the road toward the overgrown shells of houses, a few somewhat intact. A lovely peach-colored vine had taken hold of the entire front-facing wall of one of them. Olivia stepped close to examine it and caught a whiff of vanilla. The house underneath looked like it had been constructed with the same material as the steps, springy and light. She cleared away a few tendrils of vine to find a door that opened easily, as if the former inhabitants knew she would come around years later and might want to go in.

As she stepped inside, the amount of natural light surprised her. The construction material appeared to have other interesting qualities. It was transparent from the inside, letting the light stream in. Small plants broke through cracks in the floor, thriving in their fully lit shelter. The rest of the main room was unremarkable, chairs low to the ground covered in dust and a small fountain Olivia assumed was a sink. As she moved around the house, her feet crunched the thin layer of debris and crippled some plants. She could have sworn they cried out when she stepped on them.

In the next room, a table took up most of the space. It was made of a transparent material that glowed slightly with a thin, blue aura. Olivia touched it, mesmerized by its beauty. The surface lit up—some kind of computer screen more advanced than any she'd seen. It seemed to have been put to sleep in the middle of recording a written message. The writing was impossible to identify, the font trailing up and down the surface in a floral script that reminded Olivia of the sentient grass.

"Huh," she said. She tried to scroll across the page, and the message disappeared. So much for that. Moments later, a deep hum began emanating from the table, unpleasantly vibrating Olivia's teeth. It sounded louder and louder until Olivia was kneeling with her hands against her ears. It didn't help, though, because the sound was coming from inside her.

She was suddenly aware that she was dreaming. "Wake up," she screamed. If it was a dream, she could control it. "Wake up."

The sound stopped. She stood in the house with transparent walls, the humming a distant memory. She touched the surface of the computer again and found she could read the words.

189944th passage around the suns. We have decided today to leave our bodies to the land and become one with the Universe. We are finally free.

Something in the message sounded familiar, but she couldn't remember where she might have heard it before. She suddenly realized she must be on the marigold planet from her last journey. From the ground, this place didn't look like the planet she'd almost crashed into at all. It was so ordinary, she almost hadn't recognized she wasn't on Earth. Besides the shiny road, the odd building materials, and grass that seemed to sense she was there, this could have been Tireville or Indianapolis or anywhere else in Middle America.

A distant rumbling in the sky drew her attention, and dense clouds started rolling in. As much as she didn't want to be caught in a storm, she needed to explore as thoroughly as she could. If this place was as real as it seemed, she might never get back here again.

A flash of red lightning reached from one end of the sky to the other, and the outside of the house sparked as a branch of electricity glanced against it. Olivia felt it hit. Pain seared through her before everything went dark.

Olivia jolted up in bed, intense pain from the lightning still haunting her limbs. She'd never had such a vivid dream before. The pain turned her stomach, and she hurried to the bathroom to throw some cold water on her face. When she looked into the mirror, she swore she caught a faint red glow emanating from her bathroom light.

CHAPTER SEVEN

By the time Olivia finally calmed her nerves enough to eat a little more lasagna, half the day had passed. She considered calling Aerin to explain her harrowing dream, but they were putting this behind them. Olivia had promised herself to pursue as normal a relationship with Aerin as possible. That meant no aliens and no weird dreams, no matter what. Desperate for someone to talk to, she called Jody. Her friend would provide her with an objective point of view unclouded by lust. She'd get enough of that in the evening when she saw Aerin again. Jody invited her over for a late lunch, and Olivia practically sped the entire way there.

"And then this huge waterspout, like, erupted into the sky." Olivia waved her hands wildly in the air. She never was too good at interpretive dance.

"Really?" Jody absentmindedly played with a forkful of rice and veggies as she listened.

Her husband Gary had cooked a small meal for them before he'd been kicked out. Olivia was grateful for Jody's willingness to put her friends before her husband when it was necessary. They'd been married long enough that Gary knew the drill. He had driven to a nearby river to go fishing, an activity he much preferred to company anyhow.

Olivia continued. "My phone went dead right before then. Did you really not get my message? The one where I was desperately crying out for help?"

"No message. Swear. I wouldn't have ignored something like that." Jody reached for her phone to prove her point, but Olivia had already checked it multiple times. She shook her head and gestured for Jody to put it away. It didn't make sense. Her own phone hadn't saved the message either. It was as if she'd never typed it.

"So then I'm just looking up at the lake, which was all in this spout. It was so incredible, I didn't even think about what would happen when all that water came back down. Which it did."

"Christ, and you're saying Aerin was in the lake when this happened? She had billions of gallons of water crashing down on her, and she made it out alive?" Jody raised the fork to her mouth. She chewed for a long moment. "Must have had a guardian angel looking after her. You, too."

Olivia sighed. "I guess everyone else died. I didn't even see any bodies anywhere, but maybe they were washed away, or they floated out so far into the water—" Olivia stopped to take a breath. All those dead people. They'd gone so quickly.

Jody reached across her plate and squeezed Olivia's forearm. "That sounds awful."

She nodded. "The weirdest part was that none of the cars they'd come in were there anymore. Our minivan was the only one that survived. No, you know what? Maybe that wasn't the weirdest part. When I found Aerin against a tree, I turned around and saw Stanton. I know you said he wasn't there, but I swear it was him."

Jody laughed, then turned serious at Olivia's piercing look. "Oh, sweetie. You couldn't have seen Stanton."

"I saw him, Jody. I know it was him. He was hiding behind a tree, and then he disappeared."

Jody shook her head, bemused. "He was at the university all day. I saw him in the lab. I talked to him. There's no way he was in two places at once. It's impossible."

"Jody, think about it. None of this is possible. How much more of a stretch is it to believe that Stanton was there?" The look on Jody's face gave her away. "You don't believe any of this, do you?"

"You've never lied to me. I have every reason to trust you, but do you hear what you're saying? A bomb going off in a lake, disappearing people, disappearing vehicles, no damage to the town, Stanton being there? No mention of it anywhere, on any news site, no calls to the local police. It sounds like someone slipped you something."

"You think I'm crazy," Olivia said. She was glad to get it out in the open. Leaving it unsaid was worse.

"I think that maybe whatever happened to Aerin might be starting to happen to you, hon." Jody leaned back in her chair and crossed her arms. "Unless you have any other ideas, I think that's the one we have to go with."

Olivia sagged with defeat. She hadn't considered the possibility that Jody might not believe her. Though, if she'd heard the story, she wouldn't have believed it either.

"Will you just do me one favor?" she asked finally.

"Of course, anything."

"I need to see camera footage from that day. Anywhere Stanton might have been, I need to see it. Could you get that for me?"

"Normally you'd need some kind of incident report," Jody said. Olivia raised her eyebrow in challenge. "Fine. I'll get it the more fun way, princess."

"Thank you. I just need to see if there's anything out of the ordinary." She stood to leave, and Jody rose with her.

"Out of the ordinary, that's Stanton," Jody said. Olivia could see a shadow of doubt cross her face. "Well, I'm glad you came over. It's good to see you under any circumstances. Dinner tomorrow after work, usual place?"

Olivia nodded and hugged her. "Just consider that I saw what I saw, okay? Just think about it a little."

"How could I not?"

CHAPTER EIGHT

"We should definitely take Meg something," Olivia said. "For the hundredth time, she said not to." Aerin glanced in her side mirror and changed lanes. They were in her Civic on the way to her mom's house in Tireville for dinner. "Can you turn up the AC? It's hot tonight."

Olivia reached over and turned it to the coldest setting. Shivering, she shut the air vents on her side. Aerin glanced at her, waiting for a playful comeback to her temperature comment. Olivia wasn't in the mood, though.

"If it were just you, then sure, but it's me. I haven't seen Meg in forever. I should take her some flowers," she said.

"You really don't need to impress her. She already likes you."

"Well, she'll like me more when I give her flowers. It's the polite thing to do." Olivia bit down on a fingernail and looked out the window to signal the conversation was over.

Olivia had to take a gift. She'd always been fond of Meg and was certain the feeling was mutual. Just because they hadn't talked in the intervening years didn't mean that Olivia could forget her kindness and hospitality toward a gawky queer kid trying to figure herself out. Whether Meg had known then that Olivia was dating her daughter, she would have treated Olivia the same. Plus, you didn't just go to your girlfriend's mom's house with nothing in hand.

Aerin glanced over as Olivia was fixated on the side mirror. "Fine. If it'll make you stop chewing your lip, we can stop and pick something up."

"Thank you. Don't you think she'll appreciate it?" Olivia asked.

Aerin sighed. "She'll love it. Especially from you."

"Do you think she knew what was going on between us?"

"Apparently so. Before New York, she stopped by to find out why I was ignoring her calls," Aerin said.

"Why were you?"

"You know, other stuff on my mind. A bomb, you. Anyway, she told me that you were my person, and I just had to take my damn time figuring that out. Pretty sure she knew the whole time."

"The whole, whole time?" Olivia asked. She blushed as she recalled the many places around Aerin's house they'd made out and touched each other. They'd been thorough in their quest to leave no space unsullied.

"Ever since we were dating. Probably even before that."

"Damn. You think she could have said something."

"That's what I said." Aerin chuckled. "She loves you and she loves us. And that's why she insisted I bring you tonight, and also why you're probably right that you should take flowers. It's only proper."

"Told you."

Aerin rolled her eyes and squeezed Olivia's hand.

The dinner invitation had been standing for a whole month since they got back from New York. Olivia kept pushing it out with excuse after excuse. To be honest, she was nervous about seeing Aerin's mom again. It would bring back a lot of memories, good and bad, and she didn't trust herself not to dissolve in tears when Meg hugged her.

"You know the only store between us and my house is the Kroger in Tireville, right? You okay going there?" Aerin asked.

Shit. Olivia hadn't been seen in public in Tireville since she'd run into her mom and Emmanuel, her little brother, at the gas station. She hadn't seen her mother in years after being sent away to live with her grandparents, and had never met Emmanuel. That hadn't gone terribly, considering she was now in frequent contact with him, but it had been unexpected and unwelcome at the time. She took a deep, fortifying breath and kissed Aerin's hand. "What the hell. How bad could it be?"

Aerin pulled into the grocery-store parking lot, which was about half full, busy for Tireville on a Friday night. Now that you could get beer at the store, most people did, and it was cookout weather. Olivia unbuckled her seat belt and sat in the quiet car for a moment. An older couple walked past, and she held her breath.

"Ready?" Aerin asked.

"Just need one more minute," Olivia said. She looked at Aerin apprehensively. Maybe she wasn't as ready as she thought to have another run-in with someone she knew.

"Need some courage?"

"I guess," Olivia started to say before Aerin leaned over and kissed her square on the lips. In front of everyone.

Olivia pulled away, embarrassed. "Whoa. We're in public."

"So?"

"So? People don't like that here," she said.

"Last I checked, you had a little more confidence than that, and I don't give a fuck, so let's do what we always wanted to do as kids. Didn't you always dream of being able to do this in public?" Aerin asked.

Olivia thought for a moment. She had, but the reality of expressing romantic feelings toward a woman was always a little less rose-colored than in her mind. She'd seen the way people stared at her just for looking the way she did. Add PDA into the mix? Not in this town.

"Look, it's just Tireville that bothers me. I feel weird when I'm here, and I don't want to piss the wrong person off."

Aerin considered that explanation for a moment, then nodded curtly. "Okay. Let's go in then."

"Don't be mad, okay?" Olivia said. She opened the door and swung her legs out of the car.

"I'm not mad. Just a little sad."

Olivia moved close to Aerin as they walked toward the entrance and clandestinely took her hand. "How's this?"

Aerin smiled and squeezed. "Definitely a start."

Olivia shivered as they stepped into the chilly entranceway. Why was there always an inverse relationship between the outside temperature and the indoor air-conditioning? "What flowers should I get?"

Aerin walked around the small flower section and pointed. "She likes Gerber daisies. Very clichéd."

"I'll say, but I won't try to be creative here." Olivia picked a bunch of colorful flowers and headed toward the checkout. Just as she was about to turn into one of the open lanes, she froze.

"Olivia Ando? Is that you? Oh my Lord, and Aerin McLeary? What a treat, seeing you two," said a heavyset blond woman with a nose piercing.

Olivia wanted to turn around and find another aisle, but it was too late. Someone had spotted her. She put the bouquet onto the checkout belt and smiled awkwardly, trying desperately to figure out who the woman was.

"Angie! Good to see you." Aerin pushed past Olivia and hugged the woman over the bagging area.

Olivia searched her brain for a memory of someone named Angie but couldn't remember anyone. "Hi, um, Angie. Did we go to school together?"

Angie opened her mouth in mock horror, and she and Aerin dissolved into laughter. "I don't blame you for not remembering me. You had more important things to do." She winked and glanced at Aerin, who grabbed Olivia's hand and squeezed it.

"Angie used to have a giant crush on you. She told me during senior night," Aerin said.

"I was a little drunk," Angie said.

Olivia laughed, which came out a little strangled, and held tight to the checkout counter. What was happening? "That's...cool."

Angie shrugged and her face reddened. "I mean, yeah. Anyway, it's neither here nor there." She lifted her left hand and wiggled her ring finger. "Happily married."

"Oh. Congratulations."

Aerin put an arm around Olivia's waist and drew her closer. "Angie's married to Brad Lowery. Used to be the cheerleading captain?"

Olivia scrunched her forehead. There weren't any boys on the cheerleading squad. Lowery, though. The name sounded familiar. A funny, unfamiliar feeling crept up her spine. It was surprise? Elation? "No kidding," Olivia said. The Lowery she knew had been hyper-femme, always in the popular crowd. Not someone she gave a second thought to, except to avoid that entire clique.

"You two should come over. We're having a party next Friday for Brad's rebirthday." Angie nodded furiously, as if that would increase her chances of success.

Olivia chuckled. A last-minute trip to the grocery store and now this. How could she say no? "Yeah. Aerin?"

"Definitely count us in. Text me your address."

Angie nodded and rang Olivia up, a goofy smile on her face the entire time. Maybe Tireville wasn't as close-minded as Olivia assumed.

As they walked out of the store, Olivia slipped her hand into Aerin's and grinned.

CHAPTER NINE

O livia rested her head on Aerin's bare stomach and absently stroked her soft thighs. "I love this," she murmured.

"So much better than in high school," Aerin said. She ran her fingers through Olivia's hair, scratching a little at the nape of her neck. Shivers ran down Olivia's spine.

"Mm, so much better."

"We don't have to hide."

"We can do this all night if we want."

Aerin giggled. "We just did."

"See?"

Day was breaking, and Olivia had to leave for work soon. She had a high school senior starting today as part of a month-long pre-college program. The student would lay the groundwork for her own research project, and Olivia would be her mentor. Normally she loved the responsibilities that came with mentoring students, but they were far from her mind this morning. She ran a finger over Aerin's wet labia.

"Oh, Jesus. Don't start something you can't finish," Aerin said in a raspy voice.

"Who said I can't finish it?" Olivia grinned and used her tongue to make Aerin come twice.

Olivia made her way to work, leaving Aerin in her bed to catch up on the sleep they'd missed. She was exhausted, but the adrenaline of new love and constant sex would keep her mind primed until she saw Aerin again, when they'd do things decidedly unrelated to sleep. It was a vicious cycle and she savored every moment. During the eternally long days, she might not be focused on her work, but she wasn't falling asleep in her office.

At ten a.m. sharp, Olivia heard voices coming from the hallway.

"It's just there on the right," a woman said. Olivia recognized the older woman's voice. It was the building supervisor.

"Thanks, Esmeralda," Olivia shouted. She stood and walked to the doorway to greet her new student.

"No problem, Livvy," Esmeralda said. She was already making her way back down the hall.

A well-dressed young woman with short, natural hair and tasteful silver hoop earrings stuck out her hand. "Dr. Ando?"

"That's me. You must be Tameka. Pleased to meet you," Olivia said. She grasped Tameka's hand and squeezed it warmly. "Why don't you come in, and I'll give you the rundown."

"Thanks. I'm excited to be working with you." Tameka sat in the chair without pretense, and damn was it refreshing. Olivia could already tell that she and Tameka would get along well.

"Your research proposal really impressed me. Studying the impact of atonal music on the brain development of children, hm? Tell me more about that."

"Well, my uncle used to play weird music all the time for me. He said it would help me think differently, and I'm not sure if it worked or not, but I think I look at problems a little differently than other people do," Tameka said. She sat a little straighter in the chair. "If I can prove there's an advantage to growing up listening to that kind of music on a regular basis, I can help lots of kids."

Olivia wanted to laugh at Tameka's perception that, at sixteen or seventeen, she was not herself still a child, but she kept a straight face. "I see a lot of potential there. This is obviously a longer-term project, but if you come here for college, we should be able to continue working on it together."

"Yes, and there's a good chance I'll be coming here next year."

"Great. I'll give you a tour of the lab, but then I want you to go to the library and find everything you can about the effects of music on brain development. Talk to a librarian if you need any help."

Tameka nodded and stood, poised and ready to start.

"After you," Olivia said. She closed the door behind them. Her lab was a few doors down, past Jody's space full of computers of varying super speeds, books, paper, and her grad students. She popped her head in as they went by and gestured Tameka to come with her.

"Since you'll be seeing them a lot, say hi to Dr. Perralta's grad students, Beth and Stanton."

"Hi, Uncle Stanton!" Tameka ran over and gave him a big hug.

Uncle Stanton? Olivia looked between the two of them, the door, and Beth, although she had no answers to give and wasn't even paying attention.

"Remind me again why nothing makes any sense?" she said to herself.

When Tameka had finished chatting with Stanton, they continued the tour.

"Didn't realize you two knew each other."

"Uncle Stanton isn't my real uncle. He's a friend of my family's. He's the one who used to play music for me."

"Why am I not surprised?" Olivia asked cynically.

"Huh?"

"Nothing. Here's the lab." She made a note to track Stanton down and ask him some questions, like why and how he was literally everywhere, connected to everyone in her life? After a quick tour, Olivia sent Tameka to the library, then went back to her desk to think long and hard about connections and coincidences.

Later that night, as she and Aerin sipped wine and watched a mindless rom-com about some boring, run-of-the-mill heterosexuals, Olivia brought up the subject.

"Do you want to hear something weird?" Aerin nodded against her shoulder. "The new pre-college student is Stanton's niece. Sort of."

Aerin lifted her head and sat up. "That is weird. Do you think he helped her get into the program?"

"No. I don't think so. That goes through a committee," Olivia said.

"Oh. Then why is it weird again?"

"Well, listen to this. Her project is about how he played her atonal music as a kid, and now she wonders if she thinks differently. Sound familiar?"

Aerin furrowed her brow, and her expression was so cute that Olivia had to kiss her on the forehead. Aerin squealed at the touch of lips on her skin. "Okay, yeah, weird is a good way to put it. So, do you think it's connected to what happened to me?"

"Something's very off about him. He's connected to everyone—Max Pelletier, Murray, you, me, my new student. He was at the lake that day. I saw him. But he wasn't, not according to everyone else. It doesn't make any fucking sense." Olivia took a deep breath, wanting desperately to shove all this under the carpet and move on. She was trying, really, but things kept happening that made the whole situation difficult to ignore. At some point, it would be easier to find out the truth than to keep wondering. "We need to talk to him, try to get some answers. I was letting some things slide because it seems crazy to consider them, but this is one Stanton connection too many," she said.

"I'll talk to him," Aerin said.

"I'd like to be there, too."

Aerin nodded noncommittally. "I'm tired. What do you say we head up to bed?"

Olivia leaned in and kissed her, enjoying the warm sweetness of her lips. Her body was on fire in seconds.

"I need to sleep tonight, though, at some point," Aerin said.

"At some point." Olivia giggled, and they ran upstairs like teenagers.

CHAPTER TEN

A erin was about to corner Stanton. She was sure she'd pay for leading Olivia to believe they'd talk to him together. As hard as it might be to destroy and then rebuild Olivia's trust, Aerin had no choice. She needed answers from Stanton without Olivia there to impede her questioning. She was beginning to suspect that the powers she'd gained from the alien inside her had not simply disappeared; they'd been integrated into her brain so using them would be seamless, if she could figure out how. Hiding them was also easier. She needed Stanton to help her figure out exactly what was going on and what to do about it.

"And then Ben's dad turns to me and says—Aerin, are you even listening?" Zoe slammed her palm against the kitchen table. "I give up. Why did you want to come hang out here, if you aren't even paying attention to me at all?"

Aerin reached over and squeezed Zoe's hand. She'd tried to pay attention, she really had, but she had something else on her mind. "I'm sorry. I did want to see you. I mean, I do." She stopped for a moment, noticing the silence in the background. "Do you think they're done with practice now?"

"The boys? Yeah, probably. It's about that time. Why? Did you come over here for band practice? I would have told you they're playing tomorrow night at the club, so we could just go to that."

"No, no. I mean, sure, we can go to that if you want. I just needed to talk to Stanton."

Zoe scrunched her face and shook her head. "I could've given you his number. Or his address."

Aerin sighed. "I know this sounds weird, but I wanted to catch him off guard. I didn't want him to know I was coming."

"Why? Did he say something inappropriate to you? What did he do? I'll punch him in the fucking nuts if I have to for you, babe." Zoe made fists with her hands and set them on the Formica tabletop, ready to make good on her promise.

"He didn't say anything to me. I just have some questions about something." Zoe was skeptical. "An experiment we were thinking of working on together. Just wanted his spur-of-the-moment thoughts, you know?" To Aerin's relief, this explanation seemed to satisfy Zoe, and she relaxed her hands. "Anyway, if they're done, I need to go talk to him."

"Yeah, I think so. Do me a favor, though? Just tell me next time. It's cool. We could have hung out in silence or something," Zoe said. She still looked a little hurt, but Aerin brushed it off. She'd make it up to her later, however she could.

"Sorry, Zo," Aerin said as she gathered her into a hug. "I'll be back when I'm done with him."

"Done with him? Sounds like you're going to jump his bones. Have fun with that."

Jumping someone's bones sounded slightly more appealing than the conversation she was about to have with Stanton. She wasn't even sure where to begin. *Hey, Stanton, are you involved in a multi-universe alien ploy to colonize humanity through music? Do you have a little alien in your brain, too? Are you one of them in disguise?* She imagined him zipping off his human suit and revealing a blob-like gray mass underneath. She walked to the top of the basement stairs and heard the sounds of instrument cases closing amidst indistinct chatter. She would wait until Stanton walked up and corner him in the bathroom. Or maybe at his car. She should have thought this through better, but she hadn't done much thinking at all. She just needed to talk to Stanton alone before Olivia got to him. They had something in common that Olivia wouldn't understand.

Aerin felt a firm hand on her elbow and jumped at the touch. She turned to see Stanton standing behind her with a slight grin. "Startle you?" he asked.

Aerin pulled away, annoyed. "Where did you come from?"

"Went around and through the front. Didn't want to get stuck talking and be late to our meeting." He shrugged.

"Our meeting?"

He gave her a curious look and gestured between them. "This. You coming to meet me. The talk we're about to have?"

"How did you know?"

Stanton chuckled, a low, harmonic noise. "Same way you knew to come catch me off guard here."

Aerin thought for a moment. "I planned to do that."

"Indeed. And I planned to go around the front."

"I don't get it."

"Would you like to go outside?" Stanton asked. Before Aerin could answer, he was leading her toward the front door. He nodded at Zoe, who was watching the entire interaction, clearly dumbfounded. She resumed tapping her fingers on the table.

The humidity engulfed Aerin the moment she stepped onto the porch. It was due to storm tonight, an end to the oppressive dampness of the past few days. Lights from cars on the highway passed each other in the distance, and the only sound came from cicadas furiously rubbing their wings together, hoping to attract a mate. It was beautiful, Aerin thought, the way subtle vibrations could transport you if you let them. She almost lost herself in the droning buzz of sexual courtship, but Stanton brought her back with his soft, commanding voice.

"Go on. Ask your questions."

"How do you know I have questions?" Aerin asked. She realized she sounded like a petulant child but didn't appreciate Stanton one-upping her.

"I had questions once, and now I'm the one giving the answers. Plus, I've seen this conversation. This is new to you, but I know exactly what happens."

"How exactly have you seen this conversation?"

"Think about what you ate for breakfast yesterday. Easy to do, right?"

Aerin shrugged. "I guess."

"Now, think about what you're going to eat tomorrow morning."

"I don't know what I'll eat tomorrow morning."

"Why not?" Stanton leaned against the door frame.

"Because we can't see the future."

"Ah, but you and I can see the future. You've seen it before, just bits and pieces. Soon, you'll move through the future just like you move through your memories. Not all of it, of course, only what's been set."

"And how does it become set?"

"Certain choices solidify future moments in your life. It's like unlocking one door rather than another, then following that hallway to another set of doors," he said.

Aerin huffed. "So if I hadn't gone into the lake in the first place, you're saying I wouldn't be here now?"

"Can't say for sure, but that's my guess."

Aerin shook her head. If she hadn't gone into that lake, if she'd never taken the post-divorce trip to the Finger Lakes last April with Zoe, she'd never have encountered the alien energy. She'd probably still have her fledgling therapy practice and her mind. But she'd have no Olivia. On some level, it seemed worth it.

"How will I know what those moments are so I can make the right choice?"

"There are no right choices. There's only what you do and do not do."

"But I can't see anything in the future."

"You must not have done something yet, then. Maybe you still have a set of choices to make. I can't tell you what those are, but I can say that once you make one, you'll see."

Aerin was dizzy listening to this theory. As interesting as it sounded, she hated the idea that once she'd made a big choice, the next moves would be out of her control.

"Did you make sure I was at the lake setting off the explosion so you could see your future? Was that one of your moments?"

Stanton laughed. "It did turn out to be, yes. Thank you for making the choices to get there."

"Pretty selfish of you."

Stanton narrowed his eyes. "It wasn't so I could see the future. It was so the future could be better than the past. In fact, orchestrating the explosion was probably the most selfless thing I've ever done."

"Letting a bunch of aliens know that it's time to come on over and party was selfless?" Aerin shuddered. She'd thought of it before, but right now she was particularly horrified to think that her choices might have single-handedly ended the human race.

"Trust me when I say that what you helped do at the lake may have actually saved our species from certain destruction."

"It doesn't seem like it."

"Look around, Aerin. Look at the world we live in. Poverty, racism, war, climate crisis. Most of us have to fight for our whole lives to get our fair share. Don't you think we'd be better off if we all had the gifts of foresight, compassion, and logic?"

Aerin scrunched up her face. "Yeah, of course. But at what cost?"

"At any. We can't afford to wait," Stanton said.

Aerin considered that possibility for a moment. Stanton was right. The world could be better off if everyone had a bit of Rhunan in them. On the other hand, Aerin hadn't always used her gifts for good, at least not according to the people she manipulated. What if others actively courted evil? She thought back to the message she and Murray had heard in Murray's apartment. The Rhunans had ascended only after they had attained a critical mass of consciousness. No, humans were not ready for a consciousness-raising event.

Stanton laughed. "You think we're not ready."

"We're not. The residents of Rhuna One had a choice. They chose to join and ascend. In fact, as you probably know, it didn't work the first time. They had to wait until most of the species was ready. You can't force good into people. I would know. I wrote my thesis on that subject in grad school." The bit about her thesis sounded silly, but she wanted Stanton to know that she was an expert on a few things.

"Maybe not, but I've been around for two centuries, and I promise that you can create a ripple that turns into a wave."

She ignored Stanton's reference to his age. Somehow, that was the least important part of this conversation. "And then that wave turns into a tsunami under the right circumstances, and it destroys."

"Is that such a bad thing if a better world gets built afterward?"

Aerin looked up at the half moon and the stars dotting the sky beyond it. Nothing was permanent, not even the stars all the way out there, trillions of miles away. If humans continued to treat each other and their planet the same way they always had, it couldn't last. Why was she so concerned with whether the portal was opened or closed? Because the alien inside her had lied, she remembered. It had convinced her she was going to save people from drowning, and then she'd done the opposite. She couldn't trust Stanton, and she certainly couldn't trust the alien inside herself.

"I refuse to take part in bringing about that kind of change. Whether it happens will have to be up to you."

Stanton laughed. "Aerin, you're already participating, whether you realize it or not. You'll do what you are destined to do. You have no choice."

"I refuse to believe that."

"Your refusal does nothing to change that fact," Stanton said. His voice had developed an edge, and Aerin could tell he was getting exasperated. "I know you think this will be used for evil, but I assure you that's impossible. Let me show you something."

Stanton took out his phone and scrolled through his photographs. "We relocated this kid, Jackie, after her parents discovered she was cross-dressing. They threw away all the women's clothes she'd bought and locked her in the bathroom until she promised not to touch women's clothes anymore. We had one of our people convince her parents to let her go to a loving home, and we circumvented the legal system. Do you know this saves these kids years of heartbreak and days in courtrooms?"

Aerin shook her head. None of this made sense to her, and it definitely didn't sound remotely legal.

"You're concerned about the legality," he said. "Until children can exist in this world without unnecessary pain, I'm not concerned about that. When their families come around, *if* they come around, they can have their children back."

"How many people are involved in this scheme?"

"Oh, many, over the years. I've heard stories. I've even been involved in a few transfers myself, but we stay quiet. Olivia's mother, actually, she does a lot of this work because she has access to ultra-religious households across the state."

Aerin was quiet, mulling over the existence of a secret network of people who coerced families to give up their children if they deemed it necessary. How far away from child-trafficking was this? On the other hand, she almost swooned at the thought of being able to help a lot of people much more quickly than she'd ever dreamed.

"You think that by making everyone part Rhunan, things like this won't have to happen?"

"Exactly. Parents will no longer be ignorant. We won't have a need to separate families," Stanton said.

"Sounds great, but you forget that I used my powers to gamble, to coerce Olivia into doing things, to steal. I could go on."

"Yes, but are you doing those things now?"

Aerin wouldn't let herself lean into the fantasy of Stanton's words. What if he was lying to make the prospect of opening the portal sound so good she couldn't say no? His story seemed strangely matched to her own interests. This was exactly what had happened when she and Murray heard the message before the explosion. It had convinced her they would stop an explosion and mass destruction of the surrounding area, but she'd helped cause it instead. She'd have to give this situation a lot more thought.

"Aerin, don't resist it. You won't win."

She stood and glowered at him. "Don't tell me what I can and cannot resist. You aren't my boss."

In a strange, fluid motion that she was certain came from Stanton, Aerin found herself walking to the end of the driveway and into the middle of the road. Stanton's eyebrows were set in determination, and Aerin began to panic. She heard the motor before she saw the headlights coming over the hill. Pure horror gripped her as the car sped closer. Her feet wouldn't move, her legs seemed like they were attached to someone else's body, and her hands felt clammy and cold, like those of someone who knew they were about to die. The car picked up speed as it flew down the hill toward her.

"Stanton! What are you doing? Let me go!" she screamed as the engine revved louder. She barely felt Stanton in her mind, but he was there, controlling her from the sidelines. The lights were so close now that Aerin had to look away. She shook with fear, and beads of sweat rolled down her temple. She took a deep breath and prepared to die.

Then the car stopped, inches from her, its driver shielding his face from the impending impact. Stanton walked out into the street and snapped his fingers. The car disappeared, leaving Aerin standing in the middle of the road, chest heaving in and out. She wanted to throw up but swallowed the bile as she desperately tried to find enough air to fill her lungs.

"I have more power than you can imagine. I'm sorry for that. I just had to show that you cannot resist the movement that's already started. Look, I respect you, Aerin. You play an important role in the future, just as you did at the lake. But remember, you are only a pawn, like I am."

"Fuck you, Stanton. Fuck you." Her hands shook and she wanted to cry. She was too angry to do anything but swear.

"I said I was sorry."

Aerin furiously stomped to Zoe's front door. "Who are you really? Two centuries old? Bullshit." Aerin stood above him on the step and tried to puff out her chest, but inside she was terrified.

"We're the same, different ages, but the same. I became Rhunan two centuries ago. You just did. You'll learn to live with the power it gives you. Trust me. It's a gift even if it doesn't feel like one now. You're a prototype of a new human. You're going to change the world."

Stanton's predictions deflated Aerin. "Why are you telling me all this? Aren't you afraid I'll tell somebody?"

"Who are you going to tell? Olivia?" Stanton asked.

Aerin's shoulders drooped and she shook her head. If she told Olivia, she'd just confirm that she'd gone behind her back and talked to Stanton.

"Well, then. You have an important task ahead of you to ensure our people get here safely."

Stanton walked up the steps to the doorway and patted Aerin on the shoulder. "Don't forget that you have two loyalties now."

Aerin shuddered. Despite everything Stanton had promised would improve, she couldn't take the chance that it wouldn't get worse. She wanted no part in ushering in a new age and vowed to do everything she could to confine the Rhunan energy to its own universe.

CHAPTER ELEVEN

Murray Sandelman was 90 percent sure he must be dead, but he had no way to prove it. Proof was overrated, anyway. He was in paradise. He leaned back in his beach lounger and stretched his tanned legs. His veins no longer squiggled out of his thin skin like ugly green worms. His burst of white hair was now the dark brown it had been in his youth, and his hairline had been restored. Altogether, he had somehow become younger.

A waiter appeared by his side and refreshed his Long Island Iced Tea. He took a long sip and felt a little dizzy. The ocean waves gently roared onto the beach, and turquoise water twinkled with glints of sunlight. Palm trees dotted the white sand, fading in and out of focus. This stretch of beach was his alone, besides a couple of people snorkeling out by the reef.

Murray didn't want to ask too many questions about why he was here. He vaguely recalled getting off a plane, but it seemed to him like he'd taken the flight years ago rather than days. He had a nagging feeling of déjà vu. He'd been here before—drunk this particular drink and looked at these legs. He sensed another layer of consciousness, too, an awareness of everything that was to come, a sense that he would do something important.

He closed his eyes and made a wish, that he might stay here forever on this island, with its tropical fish picking at coral like little tools chipping away at concrete, its swaying palms and gentle breezes.

That night, as he reclined on the comfortable hotel mattress, Murray repeated this wish. A strange dream came to him just before he woke up. He was swimming in the reef, but he had no snorkel. He kept diving deeper and deeper, past schools of giant barracuda and rock lobsters, squid and chubs. His lungs ached as he used up the last of his oxygen, and Murray realized he would drown if he didn't get a breath soon. He wasn't afraid, though, and he inhaled the salty seawater. When he did, he was surprised to find he could breathe just fine.

Murray woke with a start, his heart pounding. His window was open, and the sea breeze was blowing through the bedroom. A rooster crowed outside his window, and he had a feeling he might just stay here forever.

CHAPTER TWELVE

I can't believe you never told me about Angie and Brad," Olivia said.

"I didn't know you would care."

Olivia sputtered. "Of course I would. I mean, I thought I was the only queer in this town for years. I don't know. It's just nice to know I wasn't."

"You knew about me. Being with my ex-husband didn't make me less queer. Anyway, I guess I should fill you in on the rest, then."

"There's more?" Olivia turned off the exit ramp and onto a dirt road. "Also, are you sure this is the right way?"

"Definitely the right way. And yeah, there are a few more. Do you remember Carrie White? She's bi. I might have kissed her during a game of spin the bottle."

"So? Lots of straights probably kiss each other during spin the bottle."

"Oh, well, she's living with her wife in San Francisco, and she flat-out told me she's bi," Aerin said. "Go right at this intersection. Also, there's James Nutter. Very, very gay."

"Go on," Olivia said.

"He's somewhere in California making gay porn films. They're actually not bad."

Olivia smacked her leg. "You've seen them?"

"Yeah, of course. He likes to play a cowboy. He's pretty good at it."

"Figures. Who else?"

"That might be it. They all came out after high school, except Angie. She came out senior year."

Olivia gulped, a question forming in her mind. "How was it for her? You know, did she ever get bullied?"

"Not great. I never bullied her, but I never stepped in to defend her, either. It was just as bad."

"But you're friends now?" Olivia asked.

"I wouldn't say we're friends exactly, more like good acquaintances who catch up when we run into one another."

Olivia nodded. She had a few people like that back in Chicago. It had been years since she'd been in town, but her acquaintances would remember her. Probably. "What is a rebirthday, anyway?" Olivia asked.

"Not totally sure, but I assume it's the date when Brad officially transitioned?"

"Oh, good. I thought I was living under a rock."

"Well, we probably both are, if that's any consolation."

Aerin twisted in her seat and pulled her phone out of her back pocket. Olivia watched out of the corner of her eye as she read something on the screen.

"What's that?"

"Oh, nothing," Aerin said.

They pulled up to the one-level house sitting on a small hill. The party streamed from the top of the hill to the bottom, trans flags and banners of every size dotting tables and chairs. A grill sizzled next to the house, and Olivia could see more people behind the haze of barbecue smoke.

"Wow. They have a lot of friends," Olivia said.

"Not surprised. They're lovely people. Let's go."

On the way up, Aerin stopped to talk to some old high school friends. Olivia carried the six-pack of beer they'd brought to the drinks table. Someone rustled next to her.

"Olivia Ando? You actually came," a man said. Olivia turned and found a guy with a scruffy beard and a backward Oilers cap. It took Olivia a moment to place him. "It's Brad," he finally said. He held out his hand to shake Olivia's.

"Oh, my goodness. I knew you looked familiar. It's been a while, huh?"

Brad smirked. "I might have changed a bit. Thanks for coming. You're a legend around here."

Olivia looked at him sideways. "I am?"

"Yeah, you were handed a crap bag of life, and now you're famous. We heard you on the radio a couple months ago."

She laughed, relieved that her legendary status was related to her relatively small amount of professional fame and not some gaffe she'd made somewhere along the way. "That's cool. I didn't think anyone listened, honestly."

"We do, for sure. I'm totally into your research, too. How's it going with the whole building a program that can read your brain waves and, like, tell you whether you actually want to date someone?"

Olivia huffed. "Wow. Nobody outside of my brown-nosing student community has ever told me they're 'into my research.'"

Brad looked around to make sure they were alone. "Tell me the truth. How did you come up with that idea?"

"Well, it's kind of a long story."

"It's totally because Aerin was with that douchebag, isn't it?"

Olivia had never felt so seen and had never wanted to run and hide as much as she did now. "Nah," she said. Brad was looking into her eyes, far past her bullshit. "Fine. I know it's absurd."

"No, definitely not. Most people deal with their shit by doing drugs or sleeping around. You actually made a career out of it."

Somehow, that made it a little worse. "Yay for me?"

"For real, bro. Plus, you and Aerin, back together. Anyway, let's crack open some of those beers you brought. I love a good IPA." Brad reached for two of them and flipped the lids.

"Thanks," said Olivia. She threw back about a third of hers right away. Must have been thirsty. "How did you and Angie meet?"

"Well, we ended up in every one of the same classes at the community college for two years, if you can believe that."

"Frankly, I'll believe anything at this point," she said.

"I still looked like how you probably remember me. Amazing hair, good figure, great clothes. When Angie and I really started hanging out, she helped me figure out that I wasn't who I wanted to be."

"There are truly not enough Angies in the world."

"Right? I think you're an Angie. I mean, not to sound meta, but you definitely helped Angie figure out who she was." He winked and Olivia blushed. What kind of alternative reality had she stepped into? She could imagine a news segment of her life: *From Outcast to Hometown Celebrity.*

Olivia smiled despite herself. "Well, glad to help. I might grab something to eat."

"We're making some dogs and burgers on the grill. Can I get you anything?"

"Thank you, but I don't eat meat."

"Not to worry. We have that, too. Come on," Brad said. He led the way to the food and tapped Angie on the shoulder. "Honey, your crush came."

Angie looked up from the grill. With a spatula in her hand, she gave Olivia a huge hug. "So glad you two could make it. I assume Aerin's here somewhere?"

"Down there talking to people I definitely don't remember. Thanks for the invitation." Olivia put a tofu hot dog in a bun. She wasn't used to all of this adoration or even inclusion, especially since she'd long assumed everyone in Tireville hated her for being different.

Brad wandered off to talk to a small group that had formed near the drinks table. Angie continued flipping burgers, and Olivia ate in awkward silence. She was about to excuse herself when Angie turned around and smiled.

"So, how are things?"

"Not bad."

"Brad didn't mention your research, did he?"

"Oh, yeah. He said he was a big fan. Nice to have fans."

Angie shook her head. "Damn. I told him not to. Did he tell you his theory about how you spent your career trying to prevent other people from heartbreak after your own breakup with Aerin?"

"Yup."

"Sorry."

"Honestly, it's finally nice to say it out loud. I'm kind of over it. I'll probably abandon it and start a new project soon."

"Now that you're back with Aerin?"

Olivia huffed. "Should have let it go a long time ago."

"No time like the present is what I tell Brad." Angie emptied the grill onto a plate and leaned back against a picnic table.

"I don't know. What if the present isn't all it's cracked up to be?"

Angie regarded her for a moment. "When else is there? There is only now," she said in a weirdly formal tone.

"She's been on a spirituality-book kick," Brad said from behind her. "Driving me nuts," he muttered to Olivia.

"Hey," Angie said.

"Brad, I might be with you on this one. I've heard enough spiritual mumbo jumbo so far in my life that I think I'm all set with that," Olivia said.

"She's fun. Can we keep her?" Brad asked Angie.

Olivia laughed freely as a warmth rose in her chest. Did she have new friends? "As much as I appreciate your offer, I haven't seen Aerin in a while. I should go check on her."

"Okay. Have fun," Angie said.

Olivia felt them watching her as she walked away. Their admiration boosted her spirits and brought back a long-lost feeling of hometown camaraderie.

Aerin was still deep in conversation with a small group of women she evidently knew well. They had never quite made it to the top of the hill and were standing on the grass next to the long driveway. Olivia lingered just behind her for a moment before feeling like a creep, at which point she bumped her arm a little.

"Oh, hey, there you are." Aerin drew her in by the waist and kissed her on the cheek. "Sorry. Time flies right by when I'm catching up with these ladies. Do you remember Tara, Steph, and Sonya?"

Vaguely, Olivia thought. Probably people she didn't particularly like, girls that ran in Brad's former circle of populars.

If she really thought about it, besides Aerin, she hadn't paid attention to too many girls.

"I'm so excited for you guys. You always made the cutest couple," said Tara, Steph, or Sonya.

"Yeah, completely adorable. It gives me hope that I'll meet the person of my dreams one day, and maybe it will be my first boyfriend," said a different one.

"Tommy?" the third one asked. She made a face.

"He's still cute," said the second.

"Who knows? It could be one of you hotties." They all giggled, and the one who'd just spoken looked a little too long at the woman across from her. Yup, that was definitely going to happen.

Olivia turned to Aerin's ear and whispered, "When exactly did Tireville become the hometown of gay pride?"

"Well, it's not, but it looks like there are just enough of us out here to have a great party," Aerin whispered back.

"Cheers to that."

A loud clanking drew their attention upward.

"Hey, can I have everybody's attention?" shouted Angie. She stood at the top of the hill and gestured for the guests to come closer. "I want to make a toast to my gorgeous husband, Brad."

A few people whooped and cheered. Brad kissed Angie on the cheek. "Aw," Aerin murmured.

"Four years ago today, my boyfriend stood on the top step at city hall in Indianapolis and held up the official documents legally recognizing him as Brad Lowery." The partygoers went wild. "Brad is the person he is today because of the love and support of his friends, new and old. Many of you were there when it really counted, and we love you for it. Thank you for coming, and please eat and drink everything because we have no room in our fridge for leftovers. Enjoy!" Angie turned and planted a loving kiss on a smiling Brad.

Olivia turned to Aerin and found happy tears streaming down her face. Angie's speech had been the perfect bookend to what was looking like a wonderful day.

"Come here," she said. She wrapped Aerin in a tight hug and kissed her cheek. "Love you."

That only made Aerin cry harder, and Olivia laughed.

"Stop laughing at my emotional craziness. It's my PMS."

"Sure, or you're just a crier." Olivia kissed her on the top of the head, inhaling the earthy smell of her hair, grounding and familiar.

Olivia and Aerin spent the ride home in better spirits than either could remember.

"I think we made some real friends at that party. Like, couple friends," Aerin said.

"Couple friends. I like the sound of that. I'm so glad I made you stop at the store that day."

"Me, too," Aerin said.

"I'm also glad that this whole alien thing seems like it's finally behind us. It's like we can live our lives now. It's fucking refreshing." Olivia sighed and settled back against the driver's seat.

A moment went by and Olivia tapped her fingers on the steering wheel, glancing toward Aerin.

"Yeah," Aerin said a little while later.

CHAPTER THIRTEEN

Stanton was halfway through a hard day's work on this refreshing springtime day in Palmyra, NY. He heaved a heavy stone from the edge of the field and launched it down a small hill. He wiped his sleeve across his drenched forehead and took a few deep breaths. He'd lost so much weight in the past few weeks that his worn trousers stayed up only because of his suspenders. He sang as he worked, spirituals he'd learned in church and from other farm workers here and there. Traveling for work every few weeks had its disadvantages, but he'd come to embrace the variety of people he met.

He'd just traveled to Palmyra on account of a tip he'd received about a possible farm job. The Smith family had fallen on hard times after the death of their son and needed an extra set of hands for harvest season. Stanton was used to the work and desperately needed the money. There were only so many jobs available to him and his black brothers and sisters in the early days of emancipation in this state, and he took what he could.

"We're breaking for lunch, Moroni," one of the Smith sons said to Stanton. He hadn't bothered to learn any of their names and had given them the surname of an Italian he'd met at a Palmyra mill a fortnight ago. Stanton tried not to mind because he would be off soon enough to work another job, one that would pay him a lot more money. He'd been able to convince the Smiths to pay him a dollar more per week than they'd offered. The pay was meager either way, but Stanton had heard they were losing the farm and couldn't spare any more. He knew there were more lucrative opportunities in his future, but first he needed to hone the newfound powers he'd received from the lake.

He'd gone there one night three weeks prior to wash the grime off his body and had stepped out a changed man. At first, he'd been scared of what had prompted thought after racing thought to fly through his mind. After some time, however, he saw how people responded to those thoughts and knew he was on to something.

A week ago he'd made his way to the Smith farm on foot. A light-haired young woman selling vegetables on the side of the road stopped him. She must have sensed his ravenous stomach that never seemed to stay full. He left with corn, bread, and pie, the latter of which she'd fetched from the farmhouse, fresh out of the oven. He'd wanted to give her something in return, but she insisted that he take the food in kindness. The interaction rattled Stanton. He'd asked her for all those things with his mind. No longer was he making his way through the world as an honest man, as he'd long seen himself. It was too easy to take what he needed. A man had to survive.

Stanton made his way to the table that Mrs. Smith had laid out with lunch. It was bean stew today, as it had been the day before. He dipped a chunk of burnt bread in the pot and brought the hot food to his mouth. It scalded his tongue, but he didn't mind. Just like yesterday, it seemed to be the most delicious food he'd ever tasted.

The farm consisted of acres and acres of corn, flax, and wheat. Stanton had seen only part of it so far, though he'd see much more by the time his work here was done. If he could get one of those horses the Smiths owned, even for a short joyride, he'd be able to get his bearings. Once he'd moved on from here, he'd find a wealthy stable owner and convince him to give up a horse.

After he'd drunk his ale, Stanton went to the edge of a small wood to relieve himself. As he was finishing up, he heard the rustling of leaves on the other side. He looked up to find a young man watching him from behind a tree. One of the Smith sons, he thought. He hadn't paid enough attention to know which one.

Stanton could taste the boy's fear from the other side of the trees well before he heard his thoughts. The kid was scared, the gaps between the trees not enough to shield him from the stocky black man on the other side. In another state, he'd be a slave, and the boy did well to be wary of a wronged man. Stanton, however, wasn't one. He huffed and was about to turn away when an awful idea formed in his mind. This was a chance to practice his powers with no one knowing. He would make the young man believe something so absurd there wasn't any chance he'd come up with it on his own, and even less of a chance that anyone would believe him. If it worked, it proved he could convince anyone of anything.

Stanton concentrated all his energy into the boy's striking blue eyes, piercing across the forest, and sent a blast of nonsensical thoughts crashing into them. He watched as the boy stumbled backward, temporarily stunned. Stanton turned to leave, hoping he'd see the fruits of his labor before his tenure here was over.

By the end of the workday, as the sun was starting to lower in the sky, he'd forgotten all about the incident. He set up camp a few feet from the house, as he'd done for a week straight. Just after he lit the fire, he heard excited squeals coming from inside the small farmhouse. How they fit all those kids in with them, Stanton couldn't imagine. He tiptoed to the window and stood to its side, listening out of sight.

"Joseph's had a vision, a vision of God himself," Mrs. Smith proclaimed to Mr. Smith and the rest of the clan.

Stanton smiled to himself, remembering what he'd put inside the kid's head. You should be scared of me, Stanton thought. Look what I can do. For good measure, Stanton projected a few more thoughts into little Joseph Smith's mind like eggs that would hatch as time went on. Joseph might forget Stanton someday, but the rest of his life would be dictated by the man who'd stood across from him in the woods that day.

Stanton retired to a blanket near a small fire he'd built. If he could use his newfound powers to fight against ill thinking, then that's what he'd do.

CHAPTER FOURTEEN

"Mm, come here," Olivia said. Freshly showered, Aerin looked unbelievably appealing putting on a floral tank top. Olivia watched her from the bed. Aerin threw her hair into an impossibly sexy, loose bun, then pressed her lips to Olivia's. The second-honeymoon phase hadn't worn off yet, and the kiss was intense.

"You don't have to go, do you?" Olivia tugged Aerin on top of her. Her cheeks were flushed, and her underwear was completely soaked.

"I do. I'm sorry. Don't you also have to go to work?" Aerin kissed her neck, biting a trail along her shoulder.

"I have a meeting tonight so I'm going in late."

"Well, we can finish this after your meeting, then."

Olivia moaned. "I might finish this right after you leave." She drew Aerin's mouth to hers again, reveling in the way their lips slid against each other, slippery and hot.

"I thought you might want to," Aerin said. She pulled the sheet down and licked one of Olivia's nipples, eliciting a surprised gasp.

"Cruel."

"Just trying to help. See you later." Aerin stood and bent down to kiss Olivia's forehead.

"Fuck," Olivia whispered as Aerin left the room. Her appetite for sex was insatiable. It wasn't as though she was deprived. Really, they'd both come four or five times just last night. She needed more, and her hand was a poor substitute for Aerin's mouth, but it would have to do.

Olivia dozed off afterward, wrapped in a sweaty sheet, satisfied and blissed out. Aerin would be back later, and they'd do the only thing either had any interest in lately. Any reason to celebrate.

A knock on the front door startled Olivia awake. She wasn't expecting company, so she peeked out the window, careful not to give the knocker any ideas about someone being home. As soon as she saw who it was, her face crumpled. The SUV was unmistakable, and the woman standing at her door was not who she had expected to see this Wednesday morning. Olivia wasn't presentable, and it would be very, very clear what she'd been up to since she last showered, so she leapt into the bathroom, turned the water on hot, and took the fastest shower she could. By the time she dried off and threw on some jeans and a tee, it was only a few minutes later. The knock came again, this time louder and more insistent.

"Okay, I'm coming," Olivia said to herself as she padded down the stairs. She took a deep breath before opening the door. "Mom."

"I'm sorry to just show up here, but we have a situation," Mariko said. She looked frazzled, her hair just slightly out of place, which was a big deal for the pastor's wife even if it would be a boringly normal look for anyone else. "Kids, come on," she yelled toward the car.

"Kids?" Olivia saw the doors open, and out came Emmanuel, as she'd expected, and a slightly older girl. Evie. This couldn't be good. "Let's go inside," Olivia said.

"Thank you for eventually answering the door," Mariko said after Olivia had handed out a round of waters. They were sitting in the living room, the kids on a love seat, Olivia and her mom on opposite sides of the couch.

"Not expecting visitors."

"Were you asleep? It's almost noon."

Olivia decided not to take the bait. "Evie, I assume something happened with your family?" She directed her question at the skinny girl who hadn't said a word since they'd arrived. Evie looked up briefly to meet her eyes and then turned away. Olivia could see tears roll down her cheeks. Her brother held Evie's hand, and Olivia loved him for it.

"Evie was...kicked out of her house." Mariko looked uncomfortable telling Olivia this unfortunate news. Good, she thought. Show some remorse for that time when you did the same thing to me.

Olivia looked at Evie, still turned away and staring out the window. "I'm so sorry, Evie. That's truly horrible. Same thing happened to me when I was your age." She glared at Mariko, who wouldn't meet her gaze. "Mom, what exactly do you want me to do?"

"You told Emmanuel that Evie could come here if she was ever in trouble."

Olivia glanced in his direction. How did her mother find out that she'd sent him that email? Emmanuel shrugged at the question in Olivia's eyes. "Yes, but—"

Mariko finally looked at her. "Did you mean it or not?"

Of course she did. Whatever she could do to help another gay kid, she would. But now? Here? She sighed. There was only one right answer. "Yes."

"Good. Then Evie must stay here with you for the time being."

Evie checked Olivia's reaction, purposely neutral, then turned away again.

Olivia looked around at her very un-kid-friendly living room. She was not at all prepared to host another living being here. She turned to Mariko. "Can I talk to you in private?"

Mariko followed her to the guest bedroom, where Olivia shut the door, then went to look out the window. The day had taken quite a turn, and she suddenly felt guilty for pleasuring herself when Evie was in the middle of a crisis, though she couldn't have known. "You want me to take care of a kid. For how long? And how long before I get arrested for kidnapping?"

"Don't be so flippant, Olivia. She's just had her life ruined. Her parents threatened to starve her until she refuses to be a lesbian anymore. She needs someone who can get her out of Tireville. Someone who knows what to do in a situation like this."

"Ah, so that's it. You think because you did this same thing to me, I know how to handle it? Passing the buck again."

Mariko huffed. "I'm trying to do the right thing."

"Then take care of her yourself," Olivia said.

"You don't mean that." Mariko walked to the window and stood next to her. "I'm trying to do the right thing to make up for when I didn't."

"You can't just make up for that. You ruined my life."

"I know what I did, but look at you. You're successful. I hear from Meg that you and Aerin are back together."

Olivia couldn't believe her ears. Meg talked to her mother about their daughters dating? What kind of alternative reality was this? Where was the homophobic mother she was sure she had?

"Please, Olivia. Martin won't let Evie stay with us. She has nowhere to go."

Olivia wasn't exactly convinced of her mother's altruism, but she couldn't watch Evie be sent who knew where to live with people she didn't know at all. "Is it legal?"

"Yes. Nobody will come looking for her."

"How do you know that?"

Mariko chewed her lip. "Trust me. They won't come for her."

"How long?"

Mariko shook her head. "I don't know. As long as you can."

Olivia realized her hands were shaking and knotted them together. "I don't know anything about taking care of a kid."

"Whatever you need, call me or Meg. We will do everything we can. You're saving her life."

She gulped, bitterness swirling in her mouth. "I wouldn't have to save her life if her parents did their job and loved their kid no matter what. It's not hard."

To her surprise, Mariko squeezed her shoulder. "I want you to know that I did my best to protect you from your father. That's why I sent you away. It wasn't because I didn't love you."

Olivia didn't believe her. "If he was so awful, why did you stay with him? Why didn't you just take me and move somewhere else?"

"I wanted to, but I was afraid." Mariko blushed, and Olivia wondered if she still was.

"Did he ever hurt you?"

"Many times."

Olivia looked into her mother's eyes and saw a fierce determination laced with pain. "I'll take care of Evie," she said finally.

"Thank you. I'll have Emmanuel get her things out of the car." With that, Mariko left, and Olivia collapsed onto the floor, burying her head in her hands. What the hell was she going to do? When she finally looked up, Evie was standing in the door frame looking worried.

"Hey," Olivia said. "We'll figure it out, okay?"

Evie didn't answer, and Olivia didn't push her. She remembered well enough what this felt like—being thrown into someone else's house like you were their problem now.

Her grandparents in Chicago hadn't exactly been supportive of her sexuality, but they'd looked the other way often enough that it didn't matter. She had a good school, decent friends, and access to the resources she needed to continue living and thriving when she hadn't wanted to do either.

When Evie went outside to help collect her things, Olivia typed out the only message that made sense and sent it to the three people closest to her—Jody, Ben, and Aerin.

Surprise. I guess I have a kid now?

Chapter Fifteen

Olivia took a deep breath and walked into one of the campus cafés. Jody assured her it was where Stanton had been heading today. At the end of summer, the campus was quiet, and the café was no exception. Stanton sat alone at a table surrounded by other empty tables. No witnesses if she made a scene. Olivia acknowledged her good luck and began to approach him.

Without looking up from his computer he said, "Hello, Olivia. Been waiting to talk to you."

Determined not to let this catch her off guard, she nodded and took the seat across from him. "Good. So have I. We need to have a serious conversation."

"Of course."

"You've got a connection to all the weird things that have happened over the past few months."

"Is that so?"

"It is. Jody showed me some footage of you at your desk at the same time I'm sure I saw you halfway across the country. Explain."

Stanton chuckled. "Ah, yes. Well, time is an illusion. Don't be too surprised if it doesn't cooperate."

Olivia just stared at him, waiting for him to go on. "So you were there. I wasn't going crazy."

"I can't confirm you saw me at a particular time and place, but if you think you saw me, you probably did." Stanton barely raised his eyes from his computer.

Olivia flushed. This was maddening. "Why were you there?"

"You mean when was I there? And when were you?"

"No, I—"

"Don't beat yourself up. You might know a lot about how the brain works, but you don't know that much about theoretical physics, do you?" he asked. Olivia shook her head. Why would she know about theoretical physics? "You learn a lot when you're living some of the more interesting aspects of quantum mechanics. Here. I'm going to order a book for you." Stanton typed away at his laptop until he was satisfied. "Okay, it's coming to your office in two days. Read it. You'll have a better idea of what's going on."

Olivia scoffed. She didn't need some book to tell her what was going on. She needed answers from the person right in front of her. "Look, we've had a pretty good working relationship for a couple of years. We've even hung out a couple of times. You don't have to be like this."

Stanton shut his laptop and sized her up. "If I told you everything right now, you wouldn't believe me. You're not ready for it. I can see you have too much resistance."

Olivia couldn't argue with that fact. "Just tell me what the deal is without being cryptic."

"Look, I helped you when Aerin needed to access the messages in her head. I'm on your side. Just read the book. It's the best explanation I can give you at this time. Now, don't you have to go prepare for class?"

Olivia remembered that she did and got up from the table. Only when she was halfway across campus did she realize it was still summer break.

CHAPTER SIXTEEN

I'll be by to pick you up in an hour, okay?" Aerin squeezed Evie's shoulder and looked on as she got out of the car and ran toward Emmanuel. He enveloped Evie in a big hug. Those two. Aerin smiled as Emmanuel led Evie inside the house. She hadn't met many kids with the maturity of Olivia's little brother. He seemed to command a quiet leadership that was the opposite of his father's abrasive manner. Zero for two, Martin's kids. Two good people who were nothing like their father, everything like their mother. Mariko was quietly undermining him at every turn, she'd realized recently. Aerin hoped Olivia might give her another chance. She wasn't a bad mother, just an effective one stuck in a crap situation.

Aerin had some errands to run in town. She had to get started with selling the house—cleaning it out and finding an agent. All that stuff she wished she could skip. Not that Olivia had invited her to move in, and not that she would agree to it this early. They were deliriously happy but still feeling each other out. Olivia was still watching for that inevitable betrayal. Aerin was double-checking every word before she said it. No, she'd get an apartment in Indianapolis, maybe close to Olivia's house on a quiet street, maybe a tiny, expensive spot on the main drag where she could quickly make up for living in a small town all her life. For the first time, Aerin felt truly free.

She stopped first at the bank to withdraw the dregs of her bank account. She stood in line for the one available teller, who was having a lively conversation with an older woman about a house fire on her street. Aerin tapped her foot and did her best not to inadvertently influence them to stop talking. She had the time to be patient, and she was trying to control her powers. It wasn't easy, especially when someone came in and stood in line behind her. She glanced over her shoulder and quickly turned forward, horrified to see Evie's mom standing there.

The last time she'd seen her had been when she had coerced Evie's parents to sign over their daughter's legal guardianship to Olivia. She'd felt dirty doing it, but Evie's life was legitimately in danger. Mariko had told Aerin about the fasts Evie had been forced to endure, at Martin's suggestion. Her parents had enforced the godly message that Evie could survive in the world only if she were not a lesbian. Aerin had done the right thing, but Evie's parents wouldn't see it that way. Shit, shit, shit, Aerin thought. She stared straight ahead until she couldn't bear it any longer and sneaked another peek behind her.

Evie's mom, whose name Aerin couldn't even remember, smiled pleasantly at her, as if she were just another stranger in line. Had Aerin been that effective in convincing her mom to forget the interaction? The thought chilled her, though it was exhilarating at the same time. She couldn't even be sure how she'd done it, though she'd succeeded. When the teller was finally through with his conversation, Aerin practically ran to the booth.

The modest ranch house she owned was her last stop. She hadn't been there in weeks for more than a few minutes. Standing in her driveway, she imagined someone else living there, raising a family, getting old, dying. The nostalgia she was afraid of didn't come, just relief to have it off her hands soon. Too many bad memories of living here with Josh and pining over the life she wanted. She'd make enough on it to be unemployed for a couple of months and pay off the credit-card debt she was building, but that didn't worry her. There was a lot of demand for licensed social workers, especially those who could secretly read minds.

In fact, she had a few interviews lined up. Next week she would start clearing out the contents of her house, and if everything went smoothly, she could have it on the market within a month. There, plan made, hands washed.

The mailbox was overflowing, and Aerin made a note to get a PO box in the city, just for the time being, so she didn't have to make the drive. She sat at her coffee table and sorted the letters, tossing catalogs and circulars without a second look. Bill, bill, fund-raiser, bill. She couldn't wait to be done with this place. As she gathered the pile of junk to throw it in the recycling bin, a small, stiff envelope fell on the floor. Aerin hadn't seen that one. Must have been stuck inside something else. She turned it over and found no return address, just her neatly inked name and address. She put it with the bills to deal with later.

Getting Evie to leave the Ando family was more difficult than Aerin had expected. Evie didn't want to go back to the city, to a town where she knew close to no one. Until a few weeks ago, her entire life was here. It hadn't been her decision to move to Indianapolis, and Aerin felt her reluctance like a pit in her stomach.

"Things going well with Olivia?" Mariko asked as Aerin sipped a glass of ice water. They'd given the kids a five-minute warning to finish up and come downstairs, though Aerin wasn't in any real rush to leave.

"Really well, yeah. We're happy. Work seems to be going well for her. I'm still looking."

"Good. That girl is stronger than anyone I know. I should have fought harder for her back then."

Aerin nodded. "She would have suffered here. This town wasn't ready for her." *I wasn't ready for her.*

Mariko nodded and smiled tightly. "Let me check on the kids."

The ride home with Evie was quiet, each of them pondering the black hole that was Tireville, Indiana, how they'd fallen in and miraculously, impossibly managed to crawl back out.

"Have fun back there?" Aerin asked when she sensed Evie was ready to talk.

Evie shrugged and leaned hard against her propped-up elbow. "It's not fair."

"Nope, honey, it's not. It totally sucks. But I want you to know that Olivia and I are here for you." Aerin wished she could ease Evie's pain beyond just covering the wound, but time would be the only balm. "Want to get ice cream on the way home?"

"Not really."

"How about we watch a movie later?"

Evie turned, her deep, brown eyes flicking. "Can Mr. Piddles sit on my arm?"

"Of course," Aerin said. They ought to think about getting her some kind of small, fluffy animal. Mr. Piddles just wouldn't do in all occasions.

CHAPTER SEVENTEEN

Thanks for taking her," Olivia said as she squeezed Aerin's hips from behind. Aerin turned around and kissed her, a kiss to make up for some of the pain Olivia and Evie shared. Maybe a thousand more kisses like that and she'd make a dent in her own guilt.

"We should get her a cat," Aerin said.

Olivia chuckled. "Oh?"

"She needs something to hold. What about a small dog? A little purse dog."

"You want me to get Evie a purse dog?"

"Yeah. Why not?"

"I'm not getting anyone a purse dog. It's a purse dog. They're not real dogs."

"Then, a cat," Aerin said again.

"If you recall, I have a bird. I can't get a cat. If we adopt anything, we should get a regular-size dog." Aerin's face lit up. "But I'm not saying we should just get a dog. I mean, she's here for now, but who knows for the long term. DCS could get involved. Then I'd be stuck with a dog. And you don't even officially live here."

Aerin grabbed her waist and nuzzled Olivia's neck. "I'm going to sell my house and find an apartment down here."

"You are?" Olivia asked. Her voice was full of surprise and hope, and Aerin was happy she'd brought it up.

"Yeah. I should be here. I want to be here with you, and now that you have Evie, I should be here for her, too. I think you could use the help."

Olivia kissed her head. "That's a wonderful idea. I got a little worried you might want to sell the house and move in here, but I don't think I'm ready." She looked away.

"I know. Aw, look at you. You don't have to be embarrassed about it. I'm not ready either. It's nice to miss you sometimes."

"You sleep over every single night. When exactly are you missing me?"

"Well, I don't have to sleep over every night. I could go home tonight if you want." Aerin made a pouty face.

"Don't go home. I like you here. But yeah, we should wait a little to move in together."

"Maybe a year?"

"We can talk about it in a year."

Aerin nodded and kissed Olivia on the cheek. "I could use your help cleaning out my place, if you're up for it," she said.

"A hundred percent, yes." Olivia took a deep breath. "I like you a lot."

"I love you, too," Aerin said before kissing her for a moment. "I have some mail to go through. Mind checking on Evie? She was a little upset in the car."

"Of course."

With one more peck on the lips, Olivia was off. Aerin flopped on the couch and emptied the wad of mail from her purse next to the book Olivia had been reading. *Flatland: A Romance of Many Dimensions*. She'd heard the title before but couldn't place it. The back said it was about a shape that traveled between dimensional worlds. Weird. Not the family dramas Olivia usually read. She moved it aside and began to sort the mail. The small envelope fell into a pile with a few other questionably junky letters.

After dinner, while Evie was upstairs changing into pajamas for the movie, Aerin and Olivia basked in the quiet comfort of domesticity. Aerin's feet rested on Olivia's lap, and the absentminded calf massage was driving her insane. They couldn't just rip each other's clothes off anymore, though. Not right here in the middle of the living room. The planning made Aerin feel like they were sneaking around, but it was necessary. They had to be quieter, a challenge on its own. Everything was a little more difficult now, but Aerin wouldn't have traded it for the world. This was what she'd always wanted, a family with Olivia, no matter how it had been formed.

"Hey, what's that?" Olivia asked. She stopped kneading Aerin's legs and leaned forward. "That letter on the floor."

"Oh, I don't know. Probably junk. Didn't open it yet." She leaned her head back and closed her eyes, wanting to drift off to sleep, but a jostling disturbed her. "What are you doing?" she asked.

"I just want to see what's in it. I don't know. I have a feeling about it."

"A feeling?"

"I think we should open it."

"Go for it," Aerin said. She rolled onto her side and tucked her knees to her chest, listening to paper tearing and then silence as Olivia read whatever was inside.

"Um," Olivia said.

"Mm? What is it?"

"You need to see this."

Aerin groaned. "Right now?"

"Right now."

Aerin rubbed her eyes and sat up as Olivia shoved the letter toward her. It was written on paper torn from a spiral notebook in small, neat handwriting. Aerin instantly recognized it as Murray's.

"Oh." She skimmed its contents.

"I know. And there's a key in the envelope."

Aerin furrowed her brow. "Huh. No date on it. He must have sent it before the lake. His apartment key?"

"Yup. Right here," Olivia said. She dropped the weathered nickel key into Aerin's hand.

"I mean, this does look like Murray's key. This letter must have been stuck in the post office for a month."

Olivia took the piece of paper back and read it again. "I guess we have to go back to New York."

"Seems like it. What are we going to do with Evie?"

They looked at each other and began to smile. "Road trip," they said in unison.

CHAPTER EIGHTEEN

A few days later, Olivia pulled two T-shirts from her drawer and stuffed them into her bag. "We've got today, the weekend, and Monday. Then I have to be back for Tameka. She's quick. I think she'll finish her research soon."

"Don't forget I have an interview at the health center on Tuesday morning. Can't miss that."

"Right." Olivia smiled.

"As for Tameka, tell her to write it all up for you. That should buy us a few more days." Aerin leaned back on her elbows and admired Olivia in her sports bra. She was still half under the tossed-about covers.

Olivia threw some underwear on top of the shirts and zipped the bag up. "I did. She sent me a draft of it last night. Really smart kid."

"Damn. Watch out, or she'll give you a run for your money," Aerin said.

"Actually, I was thinking Evie could come in and help her out. It would be good for her to meet some people closer to her own age, especially other brown girls. Plus, it will give Tameka a new challenge and buy me a little extra time to work on a paper." Olivia flopped on the bed next to Aerin and stretched out.

"You don't think, between the two of them, they'll figure out ways to make you even busier?" Aerin asked.

"Worth a shot."

"Sounds good to me, then."

Olivia smiled wistfully. "She's a good kid."

"Evie's been a blessing. We cleaned out about half the house in the last two days. I might be ready to put it on the market in a couple of weeks."

"Awesome." She hesitated. "Is Josh getting half?"

Aerin shook her head and furrowed her brow. "No. He signed the house over to me when we got divorced. He got everything else. Sorry. I thought I told you that."

"Nope. I mean, it doesn't matter. Just wondering."

Aerin rolled over and wrapped her arms around Olivia's waist, pulling her close. "You really don't have to be jealous."

"I'm definitely not jealous."

"Not even a teeny bit?" Aerin asked as she tickled Olivia's stomach.

Olivia giggled and pushed her away. "Stop. No, none. I don't care that you wasted your time with him."

"I think you do," Aerin said.

"And why would I?"

"I think part of you wishes a man had never touched me." Aerin's smile faded as she realized what she'd just said out loud.

Olivia looked at the bedpost, standing sturdily on the gray carpet, and felt the pull of gravity keeping her there when all she wanted to do was run. Or throw up. Fuck.

"I don't think that. Anymore. Jesus, I'm awful," she said.

Aerin sighed. "I'm sorry. I shouldn't have said that."

"I wish I'd never thought that."

"I know."

Olivia's throat tightened, anger and resentment she'd buried threatening to spill out. "I don't know how to make it stop. I can't stop being angry at him for getting to be there when I wanted to be."

Aerin sat up and gestured for Olivia to sit next to her. "You're with me now. He's not. I completely understand that you feel left out, but you shouldn't."

"I know," Olivia said. She felt sorry for herself, which made her feel like even more of an ass.

Aerin took a deep breath. "I've made some mistakes in my life. I'm allowed to call them mistakes, okay? You're not. To you, they're just things that happened to me in my life. They include dating people that I now wish I hadn't, but at the time it was just what happened."

Olivia nodded. What Aerin said made sense, but her feelings didn't. "Your mistake—I mean, what happened in your life affected me, too."

"How, exactly?"

Olivia shrugged. She really didn't have a good answer beyond a lingering sadness for missed years.

"Remember last time we were at Murray's?" Aerin asked.

"Uh-huh," Olivia said.

"Remember those drawings? The ones of us together? How do you think Murray knew what to draw?"

"He could somehow predict the future, with the help of your alien friends?" Olivia was trying to be snarky, but her ridiculous statement seemed true.

"How do you think he could predict the future if some things had not already been set?"

"I have no idea. Maybe it only happened because he predicted it."

"It didn't. It happened because events conspired to change the course of our lives. Neither of us could have done anything to stay together. You have to let it go. If we'd stayed together as kids, we probably wouldn't be here now."

"So, just get over my jealousy of Josh because it was inevitable?"

Aerin squeezed her shoulder. "Exactly. And don't be biphobic. Good talk."

"Asshole. I thought you had a master's degree in this stuff."

"Well, do you feel better?" Aerin asked, a smug smile on her face.

"I don't know, a little maybe."

"Then job done. Finish packing. I'll make sure Evie's ready." Aerin mussed her hair on the way out, leaving Olivia to wallow in her called-out feelings.

CHAPTER NINETEEN

Evie settled into the back seat of Olivia's WRX and clicked her seat belt.

"All set?" Olivia asked, watching Evie in the rearview.

Evie nodded and put in her earbuds. Olivia had bought her a smartphone so she could keep in touch with Emmanuel. God knows she wished they'd been invented when she was that age.

She turned to Aerin and smiled tentatively. They'd been in such a rush they hadn't spoken since their talk earlier. Olivia felt a little lighter now that she understood where some of her resentment came from. Aerin gave her a knowing look. Olivia warmed and mouthed, "I love you." Aerin nodded, her face softening. The freckles dotting her nose and cheeks and the deepening lines that ran through them were stunning.

"You're beautiful," Olivia whispered.

"I don't think she can hear us," Aerin whispered back.

"Then why are you whispering?"

"No idea. We should probably get on the road. Also, I want to marry you someday."

Olivia grinned and started the car.

An hour later, Evie had shed the earbuds, and they were playing car games. The drive to New York seemed endless, and Evie was starting to get tired of being in the car.

"I told you, I saw it," Evie said.

Aerin turned toward the backseat. "Really? You saw a white bear on the side of the highway?"

"Yes, I swear."

"Was it a white dog?"

"It was a bear."

Olivia laughed. "Just give it to her."

"Fine. One point for you. Oh, hon, Angie and Brad just texted. They hope we're doing well and would love to see us again."

"Who're Angie and Brad?" Evie asked snidely. Olivia took her attitude as a big win. She was finally starting to come around to them.

"They live near Tireville. Queer couple," Aerin said.

Evie's eyes went wide. "Oh. And you know them?"

"We'll all hang out soon, when we get back. Does that sound good to you?"

Evie shrugged, clearly trying to hide her excitement. "I guess, if you want to. Can Emmanuel come?"

"We'll try to make it happen," said Olivia.

Hours later, the magic of the trip had worn off for everyone. After switching with Aerin in the middle of Pennsylvania, Olivia drove the last few hours to New York. It was two in the morning, and both Aerin and Evie were sleeping when they arrived at a Best Western on the side of the highway in Queens. Olivia didn't want to wake them, but they couldn't sleep in the car all night.

"Come on, you two," she whispered. She gathered their things from the car and led them inside. Aerin and Evie stumbled into the lobby, leaning on each other for support. By the time they'd fallen into the two queen beds, Olivia's heart was full.

That night, she dreamed she was back in the translucent house. This time, Murray was there, too.

The sunlight streamed into the room, casting a shadow over every piece of debris that littered the floor. Olivia wondered how long this house had been left to the elements. If the sophistication of the building material was any sign, it had to be hundreds or thousands of years.

"You've found it," he said.

Olivia turned around to see Murray standing behind her. "I don't understand," Olivia said. He looked much younger than she'd ever seen him, maybe early thirties. He was smiling and looking very relaxed, tanned even. "Are you dead?"

Murray shrugged. "Yes, and no. In your timeline, maybe, but then again, you're dead in someone else's timeline. Or not even born yet."

"But I'm here." Olivia was being purposely obtuse. She was sick of this time-related bullshit she was hearing from Aerin, Stanton, Angie, and now from Murray. Could somebody just say something to her that made sense?

"I'm also here." Murray waved his hand over the luminescent table, and another message appeared. This time, she couldn't figure out what it said no matter how hard she tried to read it. It appeared she was not in control of this dream.

"You'll understand this soon enough," Murray said.

"Great, thanks. You people are a pain in the ass."

"We people are going to be everyone soon. And I promise you'll see it for the good it will bring."

"Maybe, but what if that's not what I want? What if I want to be normal, and I want Aerin to be normal? Just regular old humans."

"The great philosopher Heraclitus once said, 'change is the only constant in life.' Stop living in the past. This is your new normal."

Olivia knew, objectively, that this was true. She and Aerin had talked about moving on from the past just yesterday morning. It was much easier said than done, though.

"It was truly nice knowing you, Olivia. You won't be seeing me again, but I'll never forget you. Oh, and you'll want to trust Aerin. No matter what happens."

Olivia scoffed. "Right."

Murray disappeared, dissolving into a million tiny points of light, then fading altogether.

She blinked against the brightness, and when she could see again, she found herself seated on a couch she didn't immediately recognize.

It took her a moment to notice what was playing on the television screen—Titanic—and who was sitting next to her— Aerin. She looked at her clothes and recognized the faded Chicago T-shirt her grandparents had gifted her for her thirteenth birthday. She also wore her favorite cargo shorts that could hold change for penny candy, a can of soda, and a note from her best friend at the same time.

Aerin was saying something to her, something about how attractive Kate Winslet was. Olivia only half paid attention, tracing the bridge of Aerin's nose with her eyes, down to her moving lips. She wasn't sure when she'd started stealing glances of her best friend, but it had quickly turned into a habit she couldn't break.

"I think you're beautiful," she said without thinking. Aerin gulped and began to chew a piece of popcorn, never taking her eyes off the screen. Olivia turned away and almost felt ashamed of her confession, but seemed to remember something about how Aerin would appreciate it later. Olivia reached over to grab a handful of popcorn and caught a whiff of burnt-sugar body lotion. This smell, she would never forget.

CHAPTER TWENTY

Someone pulled back the shades and let too much morning light in. Olivia groaned and buried her face in the pillow. She felt a soothing hand on her back, rubbing back and forth. She relaxed and almost prayed for the hand explore further before remembering where she was.

"Sleep okay, love?"

Olivia breathed into the pillow as she remembered her dream. It was so real, sitting beside Aerin again in a living room ripe with tension. She never wanted to forget that feeling, full of promise and apprehension.

"What's up?" Aerin asked, her hand stilling on Olivia's shoulder.

"Oh, nothing. Just a dream I had." Olivia rolled over and looked up at Aerin. Subtle lines framed her eyes and mouth, but she was still the same gorgeous person Olivia had fallen in love with all those years ago.

Aerin scrunched her brow. "You're looking at me funny. We should get going soon. Evie and I already ate. She's down there waiting for us."

So they were alone. Olivia grabbed Aerin's shirt and pulled her down, catching her lips on the way in a passionate kiss.

"Jesus, where did that come from?" Aerin asked. Her voice came out between a whisper and a growl.

"How long can we technically leave Evie downstairs?"

"We'll make it quick," Aerin said as she cast the covers off the bed.

Seventeen-and-a-half minutes later, they raced down to the lobby, fresh-faced and showered, to find Evie chatting with a server. Evie took one look at them and raised an eyebrow.

Olivia blushed. "Sorry, kiddo. Didn't mean to keep you waiting so long." She squeezed Evie's shoulder.

"Ready, ladies?" Aerin had the valet bring the car around, and they drove the short distance to Murray's apartment.

Reggie stood at the desk, a relief to Olivia. He was one constant in a sea of weird shit happening to them.

"Reggie, hi, remember us?" Olivia asked as they walked into the lobby.

"Oh, man, couldn't forget, couldn't forget. Come to think of it, I haven't seen Mr. Sandelman in weeks. Don't know if he's in or out."

"He asked us to grab a few things for him, actually. Gave us the key," Aerin said. She pulled it from her pocket and extended her palm.

"Looks like it. Well, tell Mr. Sandelman we miss him around here."

"You bet," Olivia said. She steered Evie toward the elevator and pressed the button.

"I thought we were just going to New York for fun. Why are we going to someone's apartment, and who's Mr. Sandelman?" Evie asked.

Aerin and Olivia looked at each other, each trying to silently coerce the other into explaining. Aerin sighed with defeat when Evie caught her widening her eyes as a way to insistently plead with Olivia.

"Evie, we know this guy. He was a friend of ours, and he wants us to get some stuff from his apartment. He's not coming back to it, see, and he needs some things. It's very important that you don't touch anything, okay? Leave that to us."

"What am I supposed to do, then? You sound like my dad. Don't touch anything, don't do this, don't do that."

Olivia pulled out her wallet. "You know what? You're right. This is going to be very boring for you. I'm going to text you this address, and you can go out and explore, okay?" She pressed a twenty into Evie's hand.

Evie grinned. "Cool."

"Just don't get lost, and come back soon. Do you have your charger in that bag?"

"Yup."

"Don't talk to strangers," Aerin said.

Olivia looked at her incredulously "Aerin...Honey, it's okay to talk to strangers as long as you don't talk to creepy ones."

"Fine. Make your own rules by yourself," Aerin said.

Evie looked between them as the eternally long elevator ride finally ended. After Aerin and Olivia got out, Evie couldn't press the buttons fast enough to get back down.

"Really? You can talk to some strangers, Evie, just figure out who the creepy ones are? We're in New York City, for Christ's sake," Aerin said.

"Not all strangers are bad."

"Olivia."

"I'm sorry. I didn't mean to go over your head like that."

"Look, if we're going to parent her together, we need to have a basic understanding of the rules."

Olivia shifted back and forth on her feet in front of Murray's door. "I guess I never really thought about it like that. I mean, yeah, I guess we should, you know, parent."

Aerin looked at her quizzically. "Of course we should parent."

"Maybe I'll get a book for us."

"Truly, we don't need a book. We just have to discuss things." She put the key in the lock and turned it.

The stench that greeted them as they opened the door nearly knocked Olivia backward. "Holy fuck. What in the name of Jesus, Mary, and Joseph is happening in here?"

"Well, I assume he had some food here before he left. Guess it's still here. A month and a half later."

"Get some garbage bags. I can't be in here like this," Olivia said.

They worked for a half hour emptying Murray's rotting food, and with all the windows open, it almost smelled like a normal, old guy's apartment again.

"Wasn't expecting to do that today." Olivia coughed at the dust that had gathered as a thin film on everything. "He showed you where all his stuff was, I assume, so you be in charge. I'll look for anything else worth taking."

Aerin squeezed Olivia's shoulder. "Deal. There are some boxes in that room back there."

Olivia found the stolen EEG equipment still on the table and, horrified that she'd left it out, threw it into the back of a closet. Most of Murray's belongings were uninteresting at first glance, so she began to open drawers and cabinets. In the letter, Murray had instructed them to take anything worth having, which was annoyingly vague.

"Find anything?" Aerin asked from the other room.

"Not really. You?"

"Lots of journals mostly. You'll have to go through them with me."

"I'll keep looking, but nothing very worthwhile here," Olivia said.

She rummaged through Murray's forgotten mail and paced around the kitchen, wondering if he'd actually had an object in mind or just wanted to send them on a wild-goose chase. Something on top of the refrigerator caught her eye. She stood on a chair and sneezed at the heavy layer of dust that had settled there. It was a weathered black notebook, its pages dog-eared and wrinkled from use.

"Found something old," Olivia called.

"Coming." Aerin stepped into the weakly lit kitchen and rubbed her hands on her jeans. "What is it?"

"Here," Olivia said.

"I guess we can put this in the pile. I'm almost done in his room. Where are you?"

"Ready to get something to eat." Olivia's stomach grumbled despite the faint lingering stench of the food they'd discarded.

"I'll get Evie back here, and we'll find some lunch. Maybe we should go downtown for a bit." Aerin went to get her phone, and Olivia took one last look at the place. Should they give the key to Reggie and tell him Murray wouldn't likely come back, or keep the apartment accessible just in case?

Aerin must have read her mind. "Hey, do you think we should leave the key or what?" she asked.

"I guess we can leave it? I don't think we need anything else from here, right?"

Aerin shrugged. "Not that I can think of."

On their way out, they handed Reggie the key and let him know that they'd just had word from Murray that he was moving into a nursing home. "He doesn't need anything else from his apartment," Aerin said.

Reggie clasped and unclasped his hands. "You're sure? Should I let management know that he's vacated?"

"Yeah. He won't be back."

"I think management just needs a signed form from him."

"We'll get it to them," said Olivia.

"Okay then. Nice to see you two one last time." Reggie tipped his hat at them as they made their way into the breezy late-summer day.

Aerin reached into her back pocket for her phone and suddenly stopped walking.

"What is it?" Olivia asked.

Aerin pulled her phone out of the pocket with one hand, then reached in again with the other. When she opened it, Olivia couldn't believe her eyes. Glinting in the sun was the apartment key.

CHAPTER TWENTY-ONE

Evie met them at the car with a large bag of pick-a-mix candy.

"What do you have in there?" Olivia asked. She smiled, remembering how as a kid, she had allocated every extra penny of hers to sugar. It was part of the reason the stuff generally turned her off now.

"Gummies, chocolate, fruit things," Evie said. She held the bag close to her chest, pointedly not offering any of it to Olivia.

"Can I have one?"

Evie sighed. "I guess."

"Thanks." Olivia stuck her hand in, pulling out a few candies.

"You said one," Evie said.

"Sorry, kid. I ended up touching more than one. Didn't want you to catch my cooties."

"You're so old. Nobody calls them 'cooties' anymore."

Aerin laughed hard, a sweet melodic sound that made Olivia swoon.

"Laugh all you want, grandma. She means you, too."

Aerin wiped a tear from her eye and tried to calm down. "Ah, I needed that. Anyway, since none of us have had a square meal since breakfast, let's go somewhere and find one."

"Brooklyn," Evie blurted.

"What about it?" Olivia asked.

"I've always wanted to go there. That's where the cool people live."

"You mean the hipsters?"

"I follow this girl Donovyn from Brooklyn on Instagram. She's pansexual and in a relationship with these two girls who are sisters, and they're all brand ambassadors for Fetch Clothing Company."

Aerin raised her eyebrows in Olivia's direction, then turned her attention to Evie. "And what do you hope to do in Brooklyn? Meet her?"

Evie shrugged and looked at the ground. So Aerin had guessed correctly. "I just want to go."

"Fine with me," Olivia said.

"Okay," said Aerin. "Let's go."

Brooklyn was a lot larger than any of them had expected, and they drove through a good half hour of it on their way to the Park Slope Fetch store. They were still a mile away when the car caught up to a huge traffic jam.

"What's all this about?" Aerin peered at the long line of cars ahead and the police officer directing traffic to a detoured route.

Olivia shrugged just as a car pulled out of a parking spot in front of them. "No idea. Want to grab this spot and find out?"

"Do it before someone else does."

Music and joyful shouting filled the air as they stepped out of the car and made their way toward a barricade. Beyond was a sea of color bursting with celebration and rainbows. They'd stumbled upon a Pride parade.

"Holy cow," Evie said.

"Look at our good luck." Olivia continued into the crowd lining one side of the street. "Come on. Let's not miss anymore."

Olivia took Aerin's hand, and Aerin took Evie's. They wove through the throngs of queers until they got to the edge of the road. A trio of mostly undressed bears waved at them from a float, and Evie beamed.

"Can I get one of those hats?" she asked.

"Which hats?" Aerin followed Evie's pointing to a group of young people with odd-looking rainbow hats. "What in the world is that?"

"I don't know, but I want one."

"Okay. I'll go with you," Aerin said.

"We'll be back," she said to Olivia, leaning into her ear to project over the noise. Olivia shivered as Aerin's lips touched the sensitive skin and she clandestinely raked her teeth along the earlobe.

Olivia watched them dodge parade-goers until they reached a small stand selling rainbow crap of all varieties. She couldn't believe her good luck. A few short months ago she was alone, her work the only part of her life about which she was passionate, and now she had a partner and a kid to take care of? Not just any kid, either. Smart as hell and not going to let the injustices in her life get her down. A mini-Olivia, really.

Some whooping drew Olivia's attention back to the parade, and she laughed as a float full of drag queens with storybooks in their hands read aloud to the crowds as they went by. Indianapolis wasn't the middle of nowhere by any means, but it wasn't Chicago or New York in its liberal views. Maybe she'd look for a teaching position out here in ten or fifteen years.

As Olivia was trying to make out the titles of each book—*Heather Has Two Mommies, And Tango Makes Three*—she felt a strong grip on her elbow.

Olivia turned toward Aerin and Evie. "Back so soo—"

"Help her." An older woman in a dark-blue sundress leaned toward her ear. "Help her build it."

Olivia gulped and frantically looked around to see if anyone had lost a grandma. "Ma'am, I think you have the wrong person. Can I help you find someone?"

"Olivia," the woman said.

Olivia froze, her blood running cold on this summer day.

"You must help her build it." With that the woman released her elbow and disappeared into the crowd. Olivia tried to follow her, but she was shorter than the average Pride celebrant, and she seemed to have vanished.

"Hey, what are you looking for?" Aerin slinked an arm around her waist. They'd just come back from the stand and had clearly spent more than just a few bucks on pride gear.

"Check out my hat and my shirt," Evie said excitedly.

"Very nice," Olivia replied. She looked around, frantically trying to track the woman down.

"What's wrong with her?" Evie asked Aerin.

"Sorry. Someone just bumped into me," Olivia said.

Aerin waved her hand to get Olivia's attention. "Did they steal something? You have to be careful in the city."

"No."

"Then what is it? You're kind of freaking me out."

"You're freaking us out," Evie said.

"I, uh. You know, it was probably nothing. This random lady got confused and thought I was someone else."

Aerin looked at Evie and shrugged. "Well, okay. We got you some stuff."

Evie held up a cringeworthy piece of fabric. "We got you this hat."

"Thanks? What is it?"

"We're thinking rainbow squid. We don't know why," Aerin said.

"Yeah. We don't know why," Evie echoed. She was wearing one of her own already.

"Want to watch a little longer and then get food?" Aerin asked.

Olivia cringed as someone blew a vuvuzela nearby. "Yes, please. I think I might be hallucinating." As she turned back around, she thought she saw the old woman on the other side of the street staring at her between floats. When the next gap came, she was nowhere to be found.

CHAPTER TWENTY-TWO

Emmanuel stretched his pudgy pre-pubescent legs the length of Olivia's couch. "Was it fun? I wish I could have gone to the city."

Evie nodded vigorously. She reclined dangerously far back in Josh's old tan La-Z-Boy. "It was chill. I got candy, and then we went to a Pride parade, and Aerin bought us these awesome hats. I'll show you mine when we go upstairs."

"I can't believe how little it takes to impress this kid," Olivia whispered to Aerin. They were going through Murray's journals at the kitchen peninsula.

"Seriously. It was pretty fun, though. I've sort of always dreamed of going to Pride with you." Aerin didn't mutter the other things she'd fantasized about doing to Olivia at Pride. Full-on make-out session? That was the least risqué thing on her list.

"You have?" Olivia mockingly put her hand over her heart as her face melted with sarcasm.

"Once I finally found out what it was."

"Did you ever go?"

"Zoe and I went once. I may have ended up a little drunk and a little less clothed than when I got there."

"Oh? And how did that come to be?" Olivia asked. She slid her hand down the back of Aerin's shorts and squeezed a cheek, keeping an eye on the kids to make sure they couldn't see. Aerin whimpered.

"Someone asked nicely."

"Is that how this works? I just have to ask nicely?"

"I'm not sure that's how it works for you, but you can give it a try."

"Ew," said twin voices from the living room. They apparently hadn't been as quiet as Aerin had imagined.

"Mind your own business, prudes," Aerin called out. "Why don't you two go outside and play? It's too nice to be cooped up in a house."

"Wow, you're good at sounding like an experienced mom," Olivia said. "It's kind of hot," she whispered into Aerin's ear.

Emmanuel and Evie flew out of there so fast, someone might as well have been chasing them.

"Thank God. I've been wanting to do this all morning." Aerin pushed Olivia against the counter and kissed her so hard her own toes curled.

"Having a kid you didn't plan for is really unfortunate sometimes," Olivia said. Her lungs heaved with desire.

"We should go to bed early tonight, if you know what I mean."

"I think I might. What time is it again?"

"Ugh. I know. Not late enough. Guess we should keep looking through these," said Aerin. She kept Olivia pinned in place and reached around her to pick up a journal, pressing it against her chest. "You take this one, sexy."

"I'm not sure this is how Murray intended these to be looked through."

"Oh, I don't know. He struck me as a very dirty old man. I mean that as the highest of compliments." Aerin pulled away so they could both cool off before the kids came back in.

After an hour, Aerin noticed that Olivia was getting tired of trying to read Murray's tiny, neat writing. She was shifting from foot to foot, a dour expression on her face. "Are you seeing anything interesting in those?" she asked.

Olivia closed the journal she was reading and tossed it on the pile of things they'd already gone through.

"Okay then."

Olivia sighed and reached to touch the skin between Aerin's shirt and pants that had somehow become exposed. "What exactly are we looking for here?"

"Anything that sticks out as something Murray might want us to know. Do you need to take a break?"

"Yeah. Before I go, though, I just want to tell you I'm happy things are starting to get back to normal. No more aliens. That should be our cheer. No more aliens. No more aliens." Olivia smirked.

Aerin cringed inside. This whole alien thing was far from over, but what could she say? That she was doing her darndest to act normal for Olivia even though every bone in her body was screaming at her to give it up? Didn't she need to deal with the fact that the Rhunan energy was a part of her now?

"Every couple should have a cheer," she said. As the words came out of her mouth, she could tell they fell flat. Her throat burned with secrets. She wanted nothing more than to be the former alien host Olivia was looking for. "Go ahead and check on the kids. I'll be fine doing this for a while on my own."

"Okay." Olivia gave her a worried sidelong look that pitted Aerin's stomach.

"Okay."

Aerin flipped through a couple more journals that seemed to have nothing to offer. Just the daily happenings in Murray's life, vacations, arguments. They all looked the same from the outside. How was she supposed to know if they had anything special in them?

The old black-covered journal stood out as soon as Aerin opened it. On first glance, it seemed to be chock full of drawings, intricate and technical, like the plans for some kind of machine. She also found tiny notes around the edges of some pages that reminded her of doodles she used to do when she was bored in English class. These didn't read like emo song lyrics or those S-shaped geometric figures, though. In fact, the message within them chilled Aerin to the bone.

CHAPTER TWENTY-THREE

Aerin almost rushed outside to show the notebook to Olivia, to figure out what Murray's notes were trying to tell them together. But she didn't. Later, she would most likely kick herself for it, returning to this moment as the beginning of when everything started to collapse. Instead, Aerin went into the basement to read the notebook in private.

8/9/87: Dreamt about a machine that would facilitate entry through the portal. Drawings on this page and next from the dream.

9/1/87: Zoned out for four hours this afternoon. Vivid feeling that I had purchased long list of supplies, presumably for machine. List of items at back of notebook.

9/3/87: Can't stop thinking about machine. Voice in my head says it will open the portal at the lake. Prefer that not to happen, but coming to see I have no choice in the matter.

1/4/88: Have built prototype of machine, difficult to buy most of the parts. Tinkering to reverse its effects.

2/18/88: Convinced I've made the necessary modifications to keep them out. Reversal of amplification funnel should disperse signal instead of concentrating it. If calculations correct, portal should seal up. Reflected on page 18.

3/6/90: Met with engineering students at Columbia. They agree that my modification should have desired effect.

3/7/90: If you are reading this, you must build this machine. You are the only hope to preserve the human race.

Aerin analyzed the drawings, each sketched with such precision that she could almost see the metal shining. The machine was boxy, about a foot square, and it had a million different tiny components. Murray had quite the technical eye. She found the page where he'd erased one of the larger pieces, the funnel, and reoriented it right side up. He'd written the materials and precise sizes of each piece in a glossary in the back. None of it made much sense to her, but someone more engineering-minded might be able to help her. Zoe's boyfriend, Ben, might be just the person.

She took her phone out and dialed Zoe. "Hey, babe, is Ben around?" she asked.

"Yeah, hold on." Aerin heard her call Ben in a muffled voice.

A few moments later, she heard shuffling on the line. "Hello?"

"Ben, hi, it's Aerin. Wondering if you had like an hour or so to go over something with me." Aerin crossed her fingers and tried to force Ben to say yes, but she had no idea if it would work over cellular waves.

"Sure. When were you thinking?"

"Like, now? Maybe at your place or Zoe's?" she suggested sheepishly. Please say yes.

"Um, okay. Yeah, meet me at my house in twenty. I'll text you the address," Ben said.

Thank God. She heard a muffled argument between Ben and Zoe before she hung up. Now all she had to do was make up some excuse for why she suddenly had to go.

Olivia somehow believed her urgent need to go buy some groceries to make a romantic dinner, which wasn't a half-bad idea in the first place. She'd just have to remember to actually buy some things to cook before she returned.

Ben's top-floor apartment looked uninhabited when she pulled into a visitor's spot, so she waited in the car until he arrived a few minutes later.

"Hey there." Ben enveloped her in a hug. He gave comforting hugs, which was part of the reason Zoe was so into him. Aerin saw it. She wasn't immune to his charms.

"Thanks for doing this, Ben. I couldn't think of who else to call."

"No problem. Let's go inside and have a look."

Aerin showed him the pages and pages of drawings, and he studied them, taking notes on a piece of paper as he did.

"So what is it?" she finally asked.

"Well, see this little piece right here?" He pointed to what looked like the core of the machine. "It's supposed to be made of silver. Superb conductor of electricity. Also really expensive for that amount."

Aerin tried not to think about what this entire thing would cost her. "What does the machine actually do?"

"It looks like it's supposed to generate a strong electrical current and direct it wherever you position this side." He drew a light circle around the open side of the box and turned to the back of the journal. "Huh. I can't imagine what this is for other than to concentrate a huge amount of energy into something. I guess you could probably bore through a building with this."

"What if you turned this piece around?" Aerin pointed to the funnel-shaped object that Murray had reversed to stop the opening of the portal.

"That would probably make whatever this is much stronger. Do you see this bit right here? It would concentrate the electrons. The way it is now, it sort of disperses them. Does that make sense?"

"Kind of," Aerin said.

"Good. I'm not an expert by any means, but I've taken enough physics classes to at least guess. Hope I'm right." Ben chuckled.

"Frankly, hope you're not."

Ben scrunched his forehead. "If you want a better answer, you might try asking Stanton. He knows stuff like this better than I do."

"No, thanks."

"Suit yourself."

"Trust me. I don't want more people involved," Aerin said. She gathered up the notebook and put it in her bag.

"Things okay with you and Olivia?" he asked.

"Heh. Yeah. I'd say so."

"You sound like you just got some. Nice." He raised his hand for a high five, and she slapped it.

"And I'm getting some later tonight. Got to stop at the store on the way home, which is where she thought I was this whole time."

"Oh? Why the secrecy?"

"You know, you have to have some things of your own in a relationship," Aerin said. She barely even convinced herself.

"Yeah, for sure."

"You going back to Zoe's?"

"Honestly, I could use a break. Absence makes the heart grow fonder, right?"

Aerin smiled and patted him on the shoulder. "We do what we need to do."

On her way to the store, Aerin stopped at the library to make some copies of the pages, minus Murray's commentary. If she was going to build this machine and close the portal for good, she didn't need anyone to discover Murray's modification.

Chapter Twenty-four

It was the spring of 1843, and Sadie Foster strolled along the banks of Seneca Lake with her dearest friend, Margaret. She wore a long purple dress, the last in her possession, and carried a bag with the rest of her belongings: a brush, a few dollars, and a kerchief her mother had given her. She had bequeathed her other dress, a peach-and-cream beauty, to Margaret a few moments prior.

"What a fine day for the world to end," she said. The sun was bright, and the air smelled of freshly uncovered dirt moist from the melting snow.

"Wasn't that was he said last time?"

"His calculations are much more accurate now," Sadie said. Her voice had an edge to it she hadn't meant to add, but Margaret's disbelief in Preacher Miller's apocalyptic predictions annoyed her. His methods were sound, rooted in mathematics and a close reading of Daniel 8:14, or so her husband John assured her. Sadie had never been taught how to do mathematics more advanced than buying flour and eggs at the grocery or measuring fabric, and even then she sometimes forgot a penny or two when she left the house.

Margaret gazed out at the lake. "It doesn't seem like anything bad could possibly happen today. Just look at how the sun is making the little waves sparkle."

Sadie nodded. Margaret was right. It was a particularly peaceful day, but she believed that God would want their last day on Earth to be a peaceful one. She didn't bother arguing. Margaret hadn't believed the preacher at his first revival and had refused to accompany the Fosters to any others.

Suddenly, Margaret stopped walking. "Do you feel strange, by chance?"

"Don't be like this," Sadie said. Margaret had played this game before, pretending her soul was being sucked into Heaven right out of her body.

"No. I don't mean to jest. My skin seems to be buzzing." Margaret looked at her arms and noticed goose bumps there.

Sadie looked at her own and noticed the same, then began to feel low vibrations coming from the ground. She turned to Margaret with wide eyes. "It's happening."

Margaret was spooked. Sadie knew she had genuinely not given a second thought to Preacher Miller's ideas once the first apocalyptic prediction date had passed. Now, Margaret began to hug herself. "I don't want to die," she said with a shaky voice.

"We must prepare. Kneel here with me," Sadie said.

They dropped to their knees next to a tree and frantically looked around. Except for the vibration, nothing else seemed to have changed.

Sadie heard Margaret gasp and turned her head in the direction her friend was looking. The air seemed to undulate unnaturally in the distance, and shadowy figures began to appear. Margaret started to stand up, but Sadie caught her arm. "Stay," she whispered. If the Messiah was about to appear, she wanted to be the first to see him. Margaret crouched again and took deep, raspy breaths.

The figures faded in and out like a mirage. Sadie counted at least eight of them, but they were clustered so closely together, she couldn't really tell. Some of them appeared to be walking toward the lake. She squinted to make out their faces. Her vision wasn't perfect, but they seemed blurrier than they should be.

The closer the group of people got to the lake, the more the vibration seemed to increase, until it stopped. Sadie and Margaret watched the people walk into the water, which receded toward the middle of Seneca Lake. Sadie's jaw dropped in horror as the entire lake rose to the heavens, suspended like a glass raised in good health. Just before it came crashing back down, Sadie gripped Margaret's arm, an insane smile on her face.

"Can you believe it? Jesus has dark skin!"

CHAPTER TWENTY-FIVE

"Great work, Tameka." Olivia skimmed the bibliography of Tameka's literature review and smiled. It was about as thorough as she could have asked for. "Let's get you set up in the lab today. I was also hoping you might have room for a lab partner."

Tameka shrugged. "Yeah, sure. Is it one of your students?"

The air vent overhead came on with a whoosh, and Olivia realized she had waited too long to answer. "It's actually a young woman in my care. She's fifteen, very smart. She'll be going to Indianapolis Public Schools this fall, and I'd like for her to be involved in something here this summer, even though your internship is almost over." The more she said, the more inappropriate it sounded to thrust Evie onto another high schooler who didn't know much herself.

"I don't mind."

"You two should get along well, and you'll have an extra set of hands. It'll give you some supervisory experience you can put on your resume."

"Okay. Sounds good. When do I meet her?"

Olivia checked her watch. Almost time to eat. Her stomach had grumbled more in the last weeks than it had in years. "How about we all have lunch together today, on me."

Tameka grinned. "I never pass up a free lunch."

"That's why I like you, Tameka."

Evie met them at a sandwich shop just beyond the university campus. She'd already snagged a table by the time they got there and was working on a bag of chips. Olivia gave her a side hug and slid next to her, gesturing for Tameka to take the seat across.

"Evie, this is Tameka. Tameka, Evie."

"Great to meet you," Tameka said, putting her hand out to shake.

"You, too. I'm excited to work with you."

Olivia noticed their eyes lingering on each other, but maybe it was that neither had met someone so much like themselves before.

They ate their sandwiches between conversation. So far, Evie and Tameka seemed to get along famously. Olivia was listening to Tameka recount an interesting story when her phone rang. She let it go to voice mail, more interested in finding out whether Tameka's dog had actually been sprayed by a skunk than being interrupted.

"When he came back, he reeked. My mom was so mad that my dad left the door open. She didn't talk to him for two days." Tameka laughed and Evie's eyes lit up.

"Did you have to use tomato juice?" Evie asked.

"There's some special spray. It didn't work all the way, though. The comforter on my bed smelled like a skunk for like a whole year."

"Oh, man," Olivia said. She wrinkled her nose and remembered what Aerin had said about getting Evie a small, furry pet. After this, it would definitely not be a dog.

"Now I kind of like the smell of skunk when I catch a whiff. Reminds me of Magic." Tameka sighed wistfully. "He died three months ago."

Evie jumped in to console her, reaching across the table to put a hand on Tameka's arm. "That's really sad. I used to have a cat when I was little back in Uganda, but my parents couldn't bring her here." Evie's face fell when she mentioned her parents.

Tameka's eyes went wide. "What happened to her?"

"I try not to think about it."

"I'm sure she's fine," Olivia said. Both Tameka and Evie shot her skeptical looks. "Okay. Sorry. Just trying to help." Damn it, she'd have to get her a pet now, if only to take her mind off her long-lost kitty.

Evie passed a glance to Tameka that seemed to indicate how old and behind the times Olivia was. Olivia took the hint and finished the last bite of her sandwich. "Well, I guess I'll head on back to campus and wait for you two there. Take your time, no rush."

The door jingled as she pushed it open, and she blinked against the bright sunlight. The phone call had been from Aerin, who'd left a message to call her back soon.

"Hey there," Olivia said as Aerin answered.

"Hi. I've got great news."

"Did the house sell?"

"No," Aerin said.

"Did you find whatever Murray wanted you to find?"

"Olivia, let me tell you my news, for God's sake. I got the job at the senior center."

It took her a beat to absorb the news. "Oh, that's great. The interview after New York?"

"That's the one. I start next Monday, and get this. They're giving me a thousand bucks to relocate."

"From Tireville? An hour away?"

"Exactly."

"The same Tireville where quite a few people live and also commute to the city?"

"Olivia, be happy for me, okay? I'm a great negotiator."

Olivia looked around to make sure nobody was within earshot. "You can get me to do anything you want. That's for sure."

Aerin giggled. "Stop it. I'm on my way to look at an apartment near the university. Want to come see it with me?"

"Sorry. I can't. I have things to take care of today. Send me pictures if you like it, though, okay?"

"I will. It's a two-bedroom, so there's room for guests. You and Evie can come by anytime you want."

Olivia passed a group of white college guys playing frisbee and smiled at Aerin's enthusiasm. "You haven't even seen it yet. Hold your horses."

"The horses are off. Everything's finally working out." Aerin cut off the end of the sentence abruptly, and silence hung between them.

"Everything okay?"

"Yeah. Just remembered something I have to do. That's all. Hey, I'm here now, so I'll let you go."

"Okay. See you later. Love you."

"Love you, too." Aerin hung up first, leaving Olivia with a nagging dread.

CHAPTER TWENTY-SIX

M urray closed his eyes and let the sun warm his toned body. He'd stopped counting how many mornings in a row he'd awakened on this tropical island. At least he had a little variety in the days. When he'd taken this vacation in the sixties, it had lasted a full week, and a full week's worth of mornings was what he was cycling through. Today was Day Five, the one where he would drink three piña coladas in a row and sleep for two hours in a hammock before snorkeling the offshore reef. He'd see a squid and a handful of tiny yellow-and-black sergeant majors as he floated over a small rocky formation on the edge of the coral. And then, his favorite, a sea turtle calmly grazing in the seagrass closer to shore. If he had to pick one day to relive the most often, it would be this one.

The resort waitstaff handed him his first piña colada, and Murray brought it to his lips as he'd done countless times before. The initial sip of tangy coconut refreshed him, and he lay back in the hammock. Salty sea air danced across his skin, almost too cold when the sun was obscured by the clouds, not nearly cool enough when it wasn't. He closed his eyes to the lapping of waves against some nearby rocks and settled into a pleasant rest.

Murray woke with a painful thud and a mouthful of sand. He must have fidgeted so much that he'd overturned the hammock, which was suspended over him like a net. As soon as he'd dusted himself off and rinsed his mouth a dozen times with a glass of water, he realized something was very, very wrong. In all of the repeating events, this hadn't happened before.

Murray stumbled back up to the resort feeling disoriented and terrified. He'd figured out enough about why he was stuck here to know that any deviations meant that his timeline was off. Something in the future must have changed, or maybe he'd just been living out an island life until he figured out how to change it. He sat on the small balcony outside his kitchenette and nibbled on a banana he'd grabbed on the way out, hoping a little food might at least eliminate the possibility of low blood sugar. Deep down, he knew it wasn't the case this time. Something in his memory had unsettled him.

His latest journal, a deep-red leather notebook, rested on the nightstand beside the bed. He'd stuck a pen between the pages to mark his spot, and he opened it to reveal his last entry. Just some drivel about being on vacation without Sandi. At times he missed his wife, though the freedom that came from traveling alone was welcome. He missed her a little less here than at home, even though they'd honeymooned on this island a few short years before.

Murray lowered the pen to the notebook and began to write the date. As hard as he seemed to press the pen, he couldn't inscribe the date past the month. His pen glided over the page without making a mark. He tried again with a different pen, one the resort furnished in the room. The same puzzling thing happened, and Murray put the journal down, stymied, before he realized what had happened. He hadn't written a journal entry on this day and hadn't tried until now. He'd have to find another way to jostle the thoughts from his mind.

Murray put on his swim trunks and walked to a section of beach between two stands of palm trees. A boat rocked from side to side in the distance, but otherwise, nobody was out on the water this far from the resort. His feet sank into the sand as he made his way toward the water, and then his toe touched an incoming wave. As soon as it did, a racing stream of images bombarded him, his life going by like an out-of-control movie reel. It wasn't just his past, either. He saw things that were going to happen: buying the apartment in Queens, going to the lake, meeting Max, and finally the lake again.

The last image seemed to transport him back to the moments before he died. He rolled deep under the surface of the water, pinned so he had no escape. The sun barely penetrated this far under the surface, and Murray calmly accepted his fate. Just as he was certain this would be the end, something occurred to him, something he desperately needed to write in his notebooks. He gasped, filling his lungs with the lake water. Suddenly he was back at the beach struggling for air. Murray coughed so hard he collapsed onto his knees and threw up a little. When he finally caught his breath, he had a vision of a small machine, shiny and compact. Though he had no idea what it was for or how he'd come up with it, it dawned on him. He had to prevent someone named Aerin from building it.

CHAPTER TWENTY-SEVEN

A distant noise jarred Olivia awake in the middle of the night. Fearing the worst, she reached for Aerin and felt her warm, naked body right where it should be on the left side of the bed. She lay there for a moment and listened, but couldn't discern anything out of the ordinary. The clock read 2:41 a.m., and Olivia closed her eyes again, assuming she'd just had a bad dream. A little while later, she woke again with a start. This time, she was annoyed enough to get up and investigate.

The house was silent beyond the low roar of central air. She blindly rustled through her drawers for a shirt and some underwear. If she managed to corner an intruder, she didn't want to confront them in her birthday suit, though it would give them quite a shock. It might buy enough time for her to wrestle them to the ground or whack them over the head with a heavy object. The possibilities were terrifying and endless in the middle of the night.

She checked on Evie first. The soft sounds of slow, deep breathing emanated from her room like wisps of air. Just knowing Evie was there gave her a visceral feeling of deep contentment she'd never experienced before. As long as Evie was unwelcome in her own home, she'd take care of her as long as Evie wanted.

Downstairs was as still as a lake at sunset. Olivia checked methodically, room by room, ruling each one out. By the time she reached the kitchen, she was fairly sure she'd made the whole thing up. She stood in the glow of her under-cabinet lights and took a deep breath. It had been nothing. She took a glass out of the cabinet and filled it with water. As she brought it to her lips, something faint caught her attention from the direction of the basement. Olivia remembered with alarm the last time she'd had to investigate downstairs. It still chilled her to remember Aerin at that computer, mindlessly trawling through the deep web and unearthing decades-old messages that had led them here, to post-bomb life that Olivia hoped might be a little less complicated.

This time, though, she was certain nobody was down there, and somehow that made it a million times creepier. She took a small flashlight from her junk drawer and began to make the descent. Her heart pounded and her hand shook as she got to the bottom of the steps. At night, the basement was an eerie collection of instruments that were out of place in a midwestern suburban home. If there was ever a murder nearby and the cops saw her setup, well, they would ask questions.

The noise increased in volume as she crept into the depths of her murder basement, though it wasn't loud at all. Definitely not noisy enough for her to hear it all the way upstairs. The computer in the corner, the same one where she'd found Aerin, was lit up. As she drew closer, she could see the screen scrolling and the mouse clicking as if a ghost were controlling it. She hovered over the chair, unwilling to sit and perhaps become possessed by the musical spirit that seemed to have taken over her computer.

On the screen was a digital archive of jazz music with various clips that played in some sequence that made little sense. Olivia didn't recognize any of the pieces, although they seemed to be from well-known artists like Dizzy Gillespie and Duke Ellington. She watched for a while as the ghost did its thing, then tentatively sat, letting her butt hover a centimeter off the chair cushion. As soon as it touched the chair, the computer screen went dark.

"Damn it," she said. She'd turned off the flashlight to watch the screen, and now the basement was pitch-black.

Olivia jiggled the mouse and tapped the space bar to wake the computer up, but it was completely powered down. She finally found the power button underneath the desk, and the bright-blue welcome screen light cast the room in a sinister hue. The computer started up as normal. When she checked the browser history, however, she didn't see anything. She hadn't erased her history in a while, but then again, she wasn't surprised. These were ghost aliens they were dealing with.

She was way too keyed up to return to bed, so she tried googling everything she could think of. Alien jazz musician. Futuristic jazz ghost. Mostly she kept getting results for Sun Ra, whose seminal vision that he'd traveled to Saturn sounded strangely like a hybrid of her and Aerin's experiences. She made a mental note to do more research on him.

She searched again for mysterious happenings around Seneca Lake and examined page after page, deep into the most irrelevant results, until she found one that caught her eye. It was a historic newspaper site that had picked up a few of her keywords. The article was behind a paywall, but she immediately knew she would pay any price for its contents. Its title was *Wave From Nowhere: Geneva Drenched*, April 18, 1843.

Olivia remembered her credit-card number well enough to pay the four-dollar fee to access the article. She emailed it to herself and printed it out before she even skimmed it. She couldn't trust this machine. When she finally took it upstairs to read, she was stunned. The story went much like she might have expected if you took the events out of 2019 and put them in 1843. A giant waterspout rose into the sky that spring and subsequently splashed down beyond the bounds of the lake. Eyewitness reports recalled seeing buggies lined up along the shore that were washed away, in pieces. Two young women of some status, a little boy, and three horses did not survive the deluge. The reporter speculated that a mysterious weather event might have caused it, or perhaps the Seneca people had awakened a spirit in the lake to retaliate against recent disagreements with the United States government.

So this had happened more than once, but nobody saw it the second time? Satisfied enough with her discovery, Olivia shut off the computer and sat back for a moment in the quiet darkness. Yeah, she really didn't like it down here with the lights off. If this could be the last time she was magically summoned to the depths of her house, that would be great.

CHAPTER TWENTY-EIGHT

Olivia kept the nighttime incident to herself. She woke up past eleven the next day, and only at Aerin's urging. They were going to take Evie and Emmanuel to the science museum to see an exhibit on human bodies. The kids were already waiting downstairs by the time Olivia showered and shuffled into the kitchen.

"Sleep okay?" Aerin asked.

"Eh, not great. Pretty tired. Coffee?"

Aerin poured a mug full of lukewarm liquid out of the coffee pot and heated it in the microwave. Olivia yawned. She popped a frozen waffle into the toaster and picked a fresh peach from the fruit bowl, sliced it, and slid one of the juicy wedges into her mouth. Divine. At the very least, Aerin's presence had led to an increase in the diversity of her kitchen ingredients.

Emmanuel watched her slowly chewing her waffle creation for a moment, then sidled up to the kitchen peninsula.

"It's cool that we can hang out here now," he said.

"It is cool. I like spending time with you."

"Do you think I can drive your car a little today? Around the block?" His eyes pleaded with her, though he surely already knew the answer.

"No. You're thirteen."

"I just turned fourteen!"

"Oh, good. Then you only have two more years until I'll even let you look at the driver's seat."

"Can I just sit in it at least?"

Jesus. This kid didn't ask for much, but when he did, it was big. "With the car off and the keys nowhere near you? Sure."

He turned around and beamed at Evie, who was reading a graphic novel from the library. "I can pretend to drive Olivia's car," he said proudly.

Evie raised an eyebrow and looked at Olivia, who shrugged. "You're so boring, Emmanuel. At least ask for something you get to keep, like a gay squid hat."

Olivia chuckled and finished the rest of her waffle. The last of the coffee followed, and she rose to check on Mr. Piddles before they left.

Olivia noticed that the door to the basement was slightly ajar as she passed by. She usually left it open, or if there was something down there she didn't want Mr. Piddles to get into, she closed it. It was never halfway, unless she'd forgotten to close it last night during her foray into its depths. With her ear to the opening, she heard the sound of shuffling papers.

"Aerin?" she called.

"Oh, uh, sorry. I'll be up in a minute."

Olivia almost left her down there, but a nagging feeling in her gut kept her at the door. She detected something in Aerin's tone, a hint of dishonesty. She descended the stairs quietly and peered into the room. Aerin was standing at one of Olivia's vintage hospital beds putting papers in order. "What are you doing?"

Aerin quickly shoved all the papers into a pile and turned them upside down. "I told you I'd be up in a minute."

"Okay, but what are you doing?"

"Nothing," she said quickly. "Just looking through some papers from Murray's."

Olivia walked toward her. "Can I see?"

Aerin's shoulders sagged. "Fine. I found something in one of the journals."

"Which is?"

Aerin picked the papers up and set them out as they had been on the bed. "This is some kind of machine Murray thought would stop the aliens from migrating here permanently."

Olivia's anxiety spiked, and her heart was pounding in her head. "What do you mean, migrating permanently?"

Aerin sighed heavily, her face contorting into a painful expression. "I guess we have some things to talk about."

"Hey, are we going or what?" Evie shouted down to them.

"It's going to have to wait until after the museum," Aerin said.

Olivia scoffed. "I don't think so. You're going to tell me everything the second we get rid of the kids in there." She had a feeling she wouldn't like Aerin's explanation, but she had to know.

The ride to the museum was tense. She and Aerin didn't talk to each other, and the kids seemed to notice. They whispered quietly in the backseat, occasionally glancing toward the front as if to see if anyone had heard them. Emmanuel hadn't even asked again about sitting in the driver's seat. He knew better. He'd probably sidestepped his father's anger so often he was adept at recognizing when to keep silent. Olivia remembered that delicate dance.

Ever since Olivia had ushered them to the car so they could get to the museum as quickly as possible, Aerin wore a forlorn expression. She worried her lip the entire drive there, and by the time they'd paid the admission fee, she was so fidgety Olivia almost wanted to grab her hands to still them. Almost. She wanted to see what this was about before she committed to acting one way or another.

They instructed the kids to meet them back at the front desk in three hours, and they dashed off immediately. Olivia hoped she and Aerin would have enough time to resolve whatever this was between them. Olivia pulled her through a series of rooms— anatomy, agriculture, animal biology—until they reached the backlit walls of the medical-anomalies section. A few people wandered through the exhibit, but otherwise it was as private as they would get in such a public place.

Olivia faced Aerin and took a deep breath. "Tell me."

"I just want you to know that I never—"

"Just tell me. We'll deal with the rest later."

Aerin nodded and looked at her shoes. They were navy flats made of canvas that complemented the light-blue dress she wore.

Olivia studied them, too, both wishing Aerin would start talking and hoping she'd never have to hear this information.

"I was wrong about the bomb. Redirecting it wasn't going to stop anyone from dying."

Olivia waited for more, but it didn't come. "And? What did it do?"

"It let them know it was time to come over."

Olivia's insides crumbled like a brick wall standing up to a wrecking ball. She had so many questions, she wasn't sure where to begin. But only one mattered. "Did you know this before we got to the lake?"

Aerin's face fell, and she nodded almost imperceptibly.

Hot anger crept up Olivia's neck. "I can't believe you'd let me drive there knowing that. You didn't even give me a choice about whether I wanted to be involved."

A couple walked into the room and immediately left upon hearing their argument. Olivia supposed they were being a bit loud, but she didn't care.

"Olivia, please. I thought I was doing something for the greater good. I didn't think people would die."

"Well, they did. Murray and all those other people." She ignored the little voice in the back of her head that reminded her she'd seen Murray in her dreams recently, and he hadn't seemed in the least bit bothered by his death. In fact, he'd encouraged her to follow Aerin's lead on whatever was about to happen.

Aerin threw her hands up. "What do you want me to say? I couldn't stop it from happening, and neither could you. Does it matter who knew what information beforehand?"

"It matters to me," Olivia said quietly. It didn't really, but now that she was invested in this argument, she was compelled to finish it.

Aerin's expression hardened, and she folded her arms. "I guess I should tell you that the alien isn't gone. It's part of me now, and that's never going to change."

Olivia steeled herself against what she'd begun to suspect, which was now confirmed. "Are you serious?"

Aerin nodded dramatically. "I didn't realize it at first, but now I'm pretty sure. You've been sleeping with the enemy." She narrowed her eyes.

"Unbelievable. This whole time you never corrected me when I told you how happy I was it was gone."

"Why would I have told you when I knew this is exactly what would happen?"

"Jesus. And I'm supposed to assume you didn't coerce me into having these feelings for you." Olivia knew it wasn't true and that saying it would sting. She was angry enough to hope that Aerin hurt as much as she did.

"Fuck you. You think I don't know what you're hiding? Your dreams? The woman at Pride? Yeah, I didn't know about those until right now because I did my best not to read your mind this whole time. I've been working on controlling my powers so I don't influence you. But you wouldn't care about that because all you want is for me to be fifteen, the same person I was back then. You want to erase everything that's happened since, without remembering that what's inside me actually brought us together again. I've been trying here, and all I'm getting from you is some bullshit about how you can't trust me anymore because I've changed. Guess what? People fucking change, Olivia. I wish you would."

Olivia leaned back on her heels, dumbfounded by Aerin's accusation. She must have blinked a dozen times before she realized Aerin had left.

CHAPTER TWENTY-NINE

A erin signed the lease that evening, her eyes puffy and red. She told the rental agent she had a cold, and he handed her tissues with a side of pity. She hadn't expected him to believe her anyway. She briefly wondered whether she should even be moving to the city, but Olivia wasn't the only reason she had to get out of Tireville. That night, she drove back to her suburban ranch and slept in her bed. It had been weeks since she'd spent the night there. She shouldn't have waited so long. Perhaps some time apart earlier would have been helpful.

She couldn't bring herself to replay the conversation with Olivia in her head. She'd said some things that were probably true, but maybe she could have delivered them a little more kindly. Olivia, though, made Aerin's blood boil. She had to be the most rigid, stubborn person she'd ever met. She had a set of rules, standards she'd held onto since their high school years based on ideals and hopes. Olivia was just like that, though, all about possibility to the exclusion of reality.

Perhaps Aerin shouldn't have kept so many major truths from Olivia, but the opposite was also true. Olivia had hidden a lot of things from her. They'd both done a great disservice to each other, though Olivia hadn't seemed to grasp her role in it.

That night Aerin tossed and turned, unable to sleep alone after sharing a bed with Olivia for so long. She missed the comfort and familiarity of lying next to Olivia. She'd felt safe there in her arms, so safe she'd forgotten how vulnerable she'd become. Not that she wouldn't do it over and over again if she had the chance. Olivia had always been her kryptonite. She couldn't help the way she felt, and even their fight today didn't diminish her love. Aerin refused to believe this was the end of them. She'd stew a bit and wait until Olivia realized how boneheaded she was being and apologized.

The next morning was Sunday and the start of her mom's weekend. Aerin dropped by around eight, knowing Meg would be on her second cup of coffee by then.

"Well, look who the cat dragged in," Meg said when she opened the door.

"Hi, Mom. Just thought I'd stop by for some breakfast."

A hint of worry played across Meg's forehead, replaced by sheer happiness that her daughter was at her door. "Of course, sweetie. I'll make you some pancakes. Come in."

Meg led Aerin by the shoulders to the kitchen table and poured a cup of coffee. Aerin topped it off with more cream and sugar than she normally took, thrown off by uncharacteristic exhaustion that, for once, too much sex hadn't caused.

"Blueberries or chocolate chips?" Meg asked.

Aerin smiled and curled her hands around the steaming cup. "Some of each?"

"Of course. Are you going to tell me why you ended up here this morning, or do you not want to talk about it? I assumed you spent most of your time in Indianapolis recently."

Aerin thought back to yesterday, her anger as raw as ever. She wasn't used to feeling exasperation and pain and couldn't quite figure out how to overcome them. Her eyes welled up, despite her attempt to keep a straight face.

Meg noticed right away and abandoned the pancakes on the griddle. She wrapped Aerin in the kind of hug that should make anything okay, and she did feel a little better for a moment before realizing what had brought her here in the first place. The first couple of sobs came out just as the fire alarm started blaring.

"Oh, Jesus, I left the pancakes. Hold on, honey."

"Mom, what can I do?" Aerin asked through her tears.

"Open the door!"

"I'll turn the fan on."

"I'm shutting off the griddle."

"Throw these hockey pucks in the sink."

Finally, though a thick burnt-pancake haze shrouded the room, the alarm stopped.

Aerin and Meg looked at one another and then burst out laughing.

"So much for pancakes," Aerin said. She wiped her nose on her sleeve.

"Nothing like a little distraction. Let me get you some cereal."

Over a bowl of Raisin Nut Bran, Aerin told her mom everything. Well, sort of.

"So I left her there at the museum and got a taxi home."

"I'm proud of you, honey. You deserve Olivia's respect. I can't believe she doesn't want you to pursue your professional career. It doesn't really sound like her, if I'm being honest. Maybe she's stressed out with Evie and could use more help?"

Aerin took a sip of coffee and set the mug on the table. She felt a little guilty for painting Olivia in such an unsavory light when her actual issues were slightly more understandable. "The point is that I'm moving into that apartment, and I'm going to wait until she comes around."

Meg chewed on her lip.

"What?"

"Well, you might be waiting a long time. Some people never understand when they're in the wrong. Your father, for instance. He absolutely refused to see my parents after they yelled at him for smoking grass in their bathroom. He didn't see why they would possibly have a problem with it. He never visited them again, not even after you were born. At some point, I had to stop waiting for him to come around."

"I'm prepared to wait it out," Aerin said definitively. A moment of silence hung between them. Aerin could tell Meg wanted to say more but was afraid of overstepping. "I could actually use your help with the house stuff."

Meg tried not to act too excited. Her brow twinged, and the sides of her mouth curled up, then back down and up again. "Oh?"

"I need help hiring movers and selling the house. Do you know anybody?"

Meg pushed her chair from the table and grabbed her address book. "Sweetie, I know everybody."

Together they called a couple of Meg's contacts, and by the time Aerin left, she had a solid plan to relocate her entire life.

CHAPTER THIRTY

The museum trip had been a complete disaster. Olivia found a bathroom stall to fill with tears after Aerin left, then texted the kids to say they were leaving early. Of course they had some questions, such as "Where is the other person we came with who basically lives with you?" and "Why are we leaving after only an hour when you promised us three?" Olivia made quick work of concocting a story that she was too upset to remember afterward. Something like Aerin being called in to her new job a day early. Once they returned home and Mariko had picked up Emmanuel, she sat Evie down.

"You might not see Aerin much for a while," she said.

Evie nodded. "Did you have a fight?"

"Yeah. It was about something that we've been dealing with for a while. It had nothing to do with you."

Evie stared at her for a long moment. "Okay. Will she be back?"

I'm not sure, she thought. "I hope so."

Olivia hadn't wanted to get into it, but Evie ought to know. Aerin had been such a presence in her life over the past few weeks, and she figured that the psychological establishment would not recommend shaking the delicate foundation of a kid who'd been banished once.

Olivia ordered them pizza, which they ate mostly in silence while watching the evening news. It was possibly the most depressing night Olivia could imagine. Later, Evie shut herself in her room, surely trying to hide from the drama she'd supposedly escaped by coming to live here.

In a way, it was liberating not to have to pretend everything was okay. It wasn't. Olivia was alone in bed at seven p.m. and had no idea where Aerin was. She'd said some things, and Aerin had said some other things. She could barely understand how the argument had devolved so much in just a few short moments. She knew she'd be up all night parsing the conversation, trying to determine where she'd gone wrong. Good thing tomorrow was Sunday and her only obligation was figuring out how to be okay enough to give Evie something that resembled a normal day.

The morning broke too soon. Olivia had finally fallen asleep amidst her disheveled bedding and despite near-constant nausea. Her eyes burned with dryness. The sweaty funk coming from her clothes indicated that perhaps she ought to shower. On her way to the bathroom, she ran into Evie.

"Hey. I'm really sorry about yesterday," she said, her voice cracking.

Evie hardly missed a beat before throwing her arms around Olivia's torso. They both squeezed hard, desperate to hold on to something that wouldn't betray either of them. "I'll make us breakfast, okay?" Evie said.

Olivia nodded, fresh tears streaming down her face. "I love you, Evie."

Evie nodded back at her. It was enough, coming from a teenager.

Evie wasn't kidding about the breakfast. Her mother must have taught her some cooking skills, because by the time Olivia came downstairs, she'd assembled a mouthwatering palette of dishes. Oatmeal with fruit, nuts with a drizzle of honey, tea, vegan bacon. Olivia wanted to cry with gratitude but had to be careful to distribute her tears thoughtfully. She didn't want to turn into a crying mess Evie had to take care of. This breakfast was as far as she'd let Evie go for her.

"I was thinking we should get a dog," Olivia said between bites. She watched Evie's face light up with the controlled joy of someone who'd been let down many times before.

Evie put her spoon down and scrunched her brow. "Really?"

"Yeah. I think it would be good to have. You okay?"

Evie looked down at the table and chewed her lip. "I always wanted a dog. Mom said we would get another pet someday, but we never did. She said God didn't think it was the right time yet."

"Well, I don't give a fuck about God, so how about we clean this up and go to the shelter?" This time Evie's grin stretched from one ear to the other.

Olivia found a dog-only shelter across town. She didn't want to be tempted by cats or rabbits or little hamsters, though Mr. Piddles would have probably liked a rodent or two to play with. The shelter was having an adoption event, and the parking lot was crowded. Olivia pulled into a newly vacated spot and hoped some dogs would be left.

The door jingled as she opened it, revealing a cacophony of excited noises. She ushered Evie inside, pausing for a moment to take in the bustling lobby. Right away, the smell of disinfectant mixed with wet dog fur greeted them. A gift shop was crawling with people buying myriad dog-themed items. She made a note to stop there on the way out, whether they adopted something today or not. She could use a shirt with a cute dog on it. A peppy volunteer in a bright-pink *Adopt Our Dogs!* shirt stepped in front of them and waved.

"Hi. My name is Cindy. I'm a Dog Delivery Diva here at Indianapolis's first dogs-only rescue. What can I help you with today?" Cindy's curly brown bob bounced with each word.

"We're looking for a dog," Evie said.

"Well, you sure came to the right place. We do have some of those. Any particular dog you saw online, or do you want to browse?"

Olivia and Evie looked at each other. "Browse," they said in unison.

"Great, well, the kennel is over that way. Take a look and feel free to go inside to pet anyone who doesn't have a *Don't Pet Me* sign on their door. We had a recent shipment up from the South and lots of interest today, so not many pups left, but I have faith you'll find the perfect one." Cindy handed them a brochure for the adoption event and ushered them to the kennel.

"She's awfully happy," Olivia said when they were out of earshot. Evie giggled. "Is that how happy we'll be once we adopt a dog?"

They wandered past cages of canines, petting each one they could. Cindy was right that there weren't many left, and the choices couldn't be more different from one another. A squeaky chihuahua held its own right next to a calm pit-bull behemoth.

"What do you think?" Olivia asked when they were almost at the end of the loop.

"I don't know. I wasn't drawn to any one in particular," Evie said.

"I kind of agree. We have to get the right dog."

"Maybe we should go back around when we get to the end to see if we missed any."

Olivia nodded. "You got it." She'd let Evie make the decision, but so far, none had stood out to her either. They were all equally cute, and how could you pick when the field was so even?

They almost walked right past the small room that bookended the cages. *Special Dogs*, it said.

Olivia turned to Evie with a devilish smile. "Let's find out what makes them so special."

The room was spacious, a few dog beds scattered across the floor. A sleeping Great Dane mix caught Olivia's eye.

"Oh. My. God," Evie said from the opposite corner. Olivia turned to see what she had found and saw a fluffy white dog bed on the floor. It looked divinely comfortable—until it began to move. A soft, angelic head emerged and then serenely tucked itself back into the white mass of body.

"This is the one. Can we get it?"

Olivia stared at the dog. It looked a little worse for wear but otherwise seemed to be pretty chill. And it had fluff for days. "This is the one you want?"

"Yeah. Just look at it. It's so calm." As if it had heard them, the dog lifted its head again and stared at Olivia, whined a little, and then went back to sleep.

"Okay. Why don't you stay here and guard it while I go get a volunteer?" God, that thing was cute, but why was it in the Special Dogs room? Evie plopped down on the floor next to the dog and nodded. If that's the one Evie wanted, that's the one she'd get.

She found Cindy again and told her about the fluffy white dog. "Oh, that's Marsha, short for Marshmallow. She's a lovely lady. One of my favorites, but lots of folks are looking for something a little younger. She's nine already, but you'd never know it. She's so sweet."

She and Cindy weaved through throngs of potential adopters to get to the Special Dog room. Olivia was a little alarmed they might actually be taking an entire other animal home with them today, but she'd suggested it, and here they were.

"Let me tell you about Marsha," Cindy said to Evie and Olivia. They sat beside the dog and petted her luxurious white fur. "Nine years old, forty pounds, sweet as can be. You really can't go wrong with her. Do you have other pets?"

"Mr. Piddles," Evie said.

"He's a parrot," Olivia said. "Very well trained. Do you think she'll have an issue with him?"

"Nothing much seems to bother Marsha. If you do end up having any issues, you can always let us know, and we'll do everything we can to make sure everyone in the house is happy."

That sounded promising. "Okay, then. Where do we sign?"

Olivia's hand shook as she filled out the paperwork, each pen stroke closer to making this a reality. Her heart pounded. Evie was on to hugging Marsha and eliciting dog kisses when she pouted her lips. Looked like they would get along well. The two of them purchased enough dog food from the shelter to get them through the month and were out of there shortly after.

"Can I sit in the back with Marsha?" Evie asked.

"I think she'd be offended if you didn't." Olivia watched Evie get buckled in and waited until Marsha had stopped turning in circles to pull out of the parking lot. Marsha's hot breath tickled her neck as she drove.

"We might want to get her some dog toothpaste," she said.

Evie was too busy pointing out all the sights to her new pup. Her instant devotion was infectious, and Olivia couldn't wait to set up a run in the backyard.

"Here we are, Marsha. Home sweet home," Olivia said. Marsha barked once as if to signal her approval, and Olivia knew she'd made the right impulsive decision that morning.

CHAPTER THIRTY-ONE

Aerin's first week of work was more exhausting than she'd expected. She met with geriatric clients day in and day out, barely finding time to eat during her mandated breaks. So Zoe and Ben showing up to help her unpack was a godsend.

"I've got six things on the hardware-store list," Zoe said. She paused for a break on Aerin's comfortable white couch and scrolled through her phone.

"I have three. Guess we should go to the store soon. Let me just check on Ben."

Ben had been working on her guest room that had become a de facto storage void. Turned out there were quite a few things she'd fit in her six-room house that didn't fit in a two-bedroom apartment.

"How's it going in here?"

Ben wiped his forehead. "Not bad. Ready for a break."

"Same. We're going to head to the hardware store. You can come with or hang out here if you want," Aerin said.

"I'll crack open one of those beers I brought and see if I can't get the TV hooked up." He dropped his voice. "By the way, I've been meaning to ask you about that machine you showed me the other day."

"What about it?"

"I was hoping you'd tell me. Are you building it? Did you figure out what it's for?"

Aerin shook her head and chuckled. "I kind of know what it's for, and no, I haven't started building it yet. I'm planning on it, though. I think I'll use the guest room as my workspace."

"Aw, man, after I did all that work moving your unwanted crap in there?" Ben laughed. "I'll help you move it out whenever you need. And if you want help with that thing you're building, I might be able to find some time."

Aerin squeezed his upper arm, warmth bubbling in her chest. The past week had been difficult, but her friends took the sting away. "Thanks. I might take you up on that. We'll be back soon. Save me a beer."

"You got it."

On their way to the store, Zoe grilled her on Olivia. "So she thinks you lied to her when you were just withholding information that, frankly, you shouldn't have to tell her?" Zoe asked.

Aerin hadn't told Zoe the whole story either, but she'd told her enough. "It is a fine line, but I never outright lied to her. She did the same to me. She kept things from me."

"Get out of the street, you dumbass," Zoe yelled at a grown man who darted out from behind a car to cross the busy street.

"Jesus. Calm down."

"What? He should know better."

"Anyway, Olivia seems to think that my keeping things from her is worse than her doing the same thing, because of the nature of the thing I was keeping from her."

"Go on."

"She hasn't apologized or even acknowledged I'm alive. She clearly can't deal with me the way I am now." She didn't mention that the way she was now could be more than a little alarming to a partner. Still, how hard was it to accept that she now harbored an alien from another universe in her body?

"So she's being totally inflexible?"

"She hasn't even texted me. It's on her. She's probably waiting for me to apologize."

"She's stubborn as hell, and you seem to be able to hold quite a grudge. I have a feeling this isn't going to end any time soon."

Aerin sighed. "Maybe not. I guess we broke up. I don't really know."

"If she hasn't called you in a week, I'd say so."

Aerin felt slightly ill at the confirmation. She'd been hoping it was some fluke. Each day that passed, though, had given her more of a clue about Olivia's ambivalence toward her.

They pulled into the parking lot of Aerin's new local hardware shop and went inside. Zoe went to find stick-on hooks so Aerin wouldn't have to put holes in her walls, and Aerin looked for a new toilet seat. Once they'd amassed an armful of items, they tossed them onto the checkout counter. The sexy clerk gave Aerin a once-over as she stood back and crossed her arms.

"Let me guess, just moved into a new house?" the person asked. They had short brown hair and a slight, androgynous build. Aerin's pulse quickened. Just her type.

"Close. Just sold a house, moving into an apartment. Have to change the toilet seat," Aerin said. She forced a laugh to cover her sudden awkwardness. The checkout person rung up her items rather slowly, it seemed.

"Completely agree. I do that every time I move. Don't want to have to imagine someone else's bare butt touching mine."

Aerin chuckled and leaned closer into the counter. "Only under the right circumstances."

Zoe accidentally kicked her foot. "Oh, I'm sorry," she said.

Aerin shot her a diminishing look. "I mean, yeah, it's gross."

"That'll be $50.26. But if you want to open a rewards account, you'll get 10 percent back."

Aerin did want to open an account. She did want 10 percent back. She liked the looks of this person in front of her and figured she might stick to this store to purchase some of her components for the machine.

"Not today," Zoe said at the same time as Aerin nodded enthusiastically.

The person looked between them and then settled back on Aerin. "I'll just give you the form to take home, and then you can bring it back. I'm here Tuesday through Saturday from noon to close."

"Thanks so much for that helpful information," Zoe said with a fake smile.

Aerin paid for the merchandise and gave the clerk an apologetic smile. "Thanks," she said, ushering Zoe out the door.

"Hope to see you soon," the clerk said.

When they were out the door and out of earshot, Aerin smacked Zoe's shoulder. "What is your problem?"

"I could ask you the same thing. I was saving you from yourself."

"I don't need to be saved."

"Um, you're flirting with some hottie, and you don't even know for sure whether you're still in a relationship with the person you've been pining over for basically your whole life."

Aerin pouted. Zoe was kind of right, but she wasn't about to admit it. "I'm allowed to flirt."

"Uh-huh. You almost gave them your number on that card application. Guess who was probably going to call you later."

"So?" Aerin folded her arms. She was feeling defiant for no reason at all. Maybe this whole business with Olivia was finally getting to her.

"So you have a bit of a history of infidelity. If you ever want to fix your relationship with Olivia, you should think twice."

"But you said we basically broke up."

"I'm just trying to support you. I said that because I thought that's what you wanted to hear. But shit got real in there, and I just think you should make sure. That's all."

Aerin sighed and shuffled to the car. "Fine."

"Call Olivia."

"No. Ball's in her court. She has to call first."

Zoe groaned. "You two are infuriating."

CHAPTER THIRTY-TWO

By the end of September, Olivia, Evie, Mr. Piddles, and Marsha had settled into a routine. Olivia would drop Evie off at school every morning, then head to the office, where she would wonder what became of her life for eight hours. Sometimes she halfheartedly worked on drawing up a new research project or taught a class. Since the museum, Aerin hadn't called or come back for her stuff, so. Olivia assumed it was over. Aerin didn't want to be with her anymore, which was completely fine because Olivia wanted to date someone who was 100 percent human and who didn't keep secrets from her.

She'd concluded that their relationship was doomed to fail. Had Aerin told her immediately after the explosion that she still had alien in her, Olivia might have come around. Aerin's failure to do that made her call into question their entire time together. Which moments were genuine and which weren't? They'd all felt real, but could she trust her feelings when she knew mind control might be involved?

Stanton stopped by often to check in on her. She was polite but not enthusiastic about his visits. She'd tried to get answers again and again, but every time he popped his head in, she forgot what she wanted to ask. He asked her about the book once or twice, and Olivia pretended not to have read it. Interdimensional travel belonged in fiction, not real life, though it did explain a few things, like why nobody else had seen the explosion and how Stanton could be in two places at once. Eventually, she resigned herself to being glad she didn't have to deal directly with the alien debacle anymore.

Tameka had left weeks ago with an offer to return the following summer. She and Evie ended up at the same high school and saw each other most days. In fact, Evie was going to her house tonight for a sleepover, which meant Olivia would be spending the night alone for the first time since Aerin left.

It had been a while since she'd done experiments on Mr. Piddles, so she set one up when she got home, more for distraction than results.

"Olivia, spend time with me," he said when she opened the door to his room.

"We're going to do that, bud. Mom's going to do an experiment with you. Come." Mr. Piddles flew to her shoulder and nipped her on the ear the entire way to the basement. Marsha tried to follow, but Olivia shooed her upstairs so she wouldn't interfere.

"What do you want to do today? Images, sounds, syntax?" Olivia gave him the usual choices. He hopped to the perch and nodded.

"Sounds. Treat."

"You get a treat when you're done. Nice try, though. I will give you scritches." She nuzzled Mr. Piddles and stroked his head while he cooed. Between taking care of Evie and Marsha, plus her budding self-diagnosed depression, she'd been a little neglectful of her bird. "I promise I'll spend more time with you, okay?"

"Marsha should go," he said.

Olivia chuckled. "Marsha's not going anywhere."

"Aerin should come back."

"Yeah," she whispered. Despite constant justification of her spiteful words, she secretly agreed with him. If only it were that simple.

Olivia put on a series of sounds and had Mr. Piddles mimic them, then describe what they were. They were on number four, a herd of elephants in mourning, when Olivia's phone began to ring.

She let it go to voice mail once, then twice. The third time, she figured she ought to at least see who was calling.

The number didn't look familiar, but the location did. She knew only one person in Montreal.

"Hello?"

"Dr. Ando? This is Dr. Pelletier." Max sounded shaken, his words rushed and timbre higher than she remembered.

"Hi, Max. What's going on?"

"Forgive me for calling out of the blue, but I had to tell you something. An electrical fire started in my study and burned the upstairs of my house."

Olivia put her hand over her mouth. "I'm so sorry. Are you okay? Is everyone okay?"

"Yes, everyone is fine. It was while we were out. The fire isn't the point of my story, though." What could he possibly tell her that was more sensational? "It was what was not burned that unnerved me," Max said.

"What was it?"

Max took a deep breath. "All of the notes I had from when Mr. Sandelman shared his story with me. I hadn't even remembered I'd kept them. The strange thing was that everything else around them was burned, but they are pristine. Completely untouched."

Olivia's heart sank. It seemed that she couldn't do anything to escape this narrative. It came at her from all directions and popped up at the most inopportune times. Aerin. The woman at Pride. Her dreams. Now this.

"Hello?"

"Yes," Olivia said.

"I will send them to you for your investigation. I don't want them in my house any longer."

Olivia couldn't blame him. She didn't want them either. "Okay."

"Good. Have you heard from Murray lately?"

Olivia faltered. Max knew too little, and Olivia didn't have the patience to bring him up to speed. "No. I haven't heard anything."

"I hope he's doing okay."

She couldn't lie out loud, so she just nodded and hoped Max would somehow get the message.

"Well, I'll send them to you, then. Good luck with your research."

"Thank you. I'm sorry about your house."

"It is just a house. We're okay," he said.

"Bye, Max."

"Bye."

How he could be so damn levelheaded when he'd lost half his house threw Olivia for a loop. She could barely go an hour without thinking about Aerin, and she was just a call away.

That night, as Marsha snuggled up in bed with her, Olivia dreamt about the old woman who had caught her in the parade crowd. "Help her," the woman said over and over. "Help her."

CHAPTER THIRTY-THREE

How much is pure silver again?" Aerin asked the proprietor at Indianapolis's top rare-coin dealer. A banner in the front window assured her of its status.

"Today it's 598 dollars per kilo," said the dealer.

"Hm."

"It's a good investment, but the price fluctuates more than the price of gold. That can work either for or against you. Right now, it's neutral."

Aerin hadn't been clear about her intentions for the metal. "Is it easy to melt it down and form it into whatever shape I want?"

"Of course, but you'll need the equipment to form it into jewelry," the man said. He pushed his round spectacles to the bridge of his nose.

"I'm not making jewelry. It's a machine component. I'm a bit of an inventor, and I'm trying out a new gadget." Bit of an inventor?

"Ah."

"So should I go somewhere else?"

"It will likely be easier to get it formed to your specifications if you don't have the equipment to mold it yourself. There are quite a few industrial-metal companies around here. Give one of them a call."

"Thanks. Do you have an idea of how much it will cost?"

"Same base price but add a bit for the quality and a bit more for forming it into whatever shape you're looking for."

"Great," Aerin said. She took out a photocopy of the list of components Murray had made and wrote "find industrial-metal company" next to the silver cone. She let her shoulders slump. This was a hopeless undertaking, and she'd only begun to collect materials. If this was how she'd have to track down the other three-hundred-and-six components, this machine would never be built. For a fleeting moment, she considered whether that might be better. No, Murray was right. She should close the portal if she could. Nobody else should be subjected to the mysterious and unnerving condition of being part alien.

Aerin thanked the man and left, propelling herself down the street in no particular direction. She'd seen all her clients for the day and left early, so even the busiest parts of town weren't that crowded. Though the temperature was getting colder each day, a few people sat at small tables outside a café across the street. Aerin's stomach grumbled as she crossed the road.

The small café offered a mouthwatering assortment of pastries and quiches. Aerin ordered a spinach-and-feta quiche with a side of hot coffee. She grabbed a complimentary wellness magazine because it had a picture of lavender on the cover. Lavender was a nice, calming plant, and right now she wished she had more of it in her life.

She quickly finished flipping through the magazine and drained the last drop of coffee, then sat back in her chair, wondering what to do next. A trip to the hardware store could be in order, though she might get started on that industrial-metals company. The breadth of the project depressed her. She'd never get it done. She barely knew what a pair of needle-nose pliers looked like, let alone the hundreds of individual components those pliers would tweak.

As she stood to leave, a bulletin board in the corner caught her eye, its contents overlapping pieces of torn color. A new bright-yellow flyer had been added to the bottom left so that it hung far below the bottom of the board. She could read two words from across the room: *Need Help?*

"Yes," Aerin said to herself. Upon closer inspection, Aerin saw that the sign was advertising a handyperson. Precisely what she could use right now to help with the machine. She tore off a slip of paper and put it in her pocket.

The moment she got outside, she dialed the number. The call went to voice mail, and she left her name and number, but no description of her unusual request just yet. She at least wanted a chance to convince them before they went running in the other direction.

A few minutes later, her phone buzzed.

"Hello?"

"Hi. This is Cassie. You called about my handyman services?" The voice on the other end sounded vaguely familiar, but she couldn't place it.

"Yes. I have a bit of a strange request, more of a longer-term project."

"No problem. I do bigger projects all the time. What are you looking to have done?"

Aerin had no idea how to answer that question. Fix a hole between two universes? That wouldn't go over well. "I'm actually building something complicated and need help procuring all the parts. Is that something you can help with?"

"Yeah, probably. So, you just want someone who knows where to find components?"

Aerin bit her lip. "And to go get them for me."

"That doesn't sound like it will take too long."

"It has over three hundred components, and I have no idea where to find most of them."

Cassie made a concerned noise. "I see how that could be longer term. I'm happy to help, though. My rate is thirty dollars an hour, plus mileage, if I'm driving to a lot of different places. Will that work for you?"

Aerin cringed. She couldn't afford not to if she was going to get this done sometime this century. "That should work. When can you come by to discuss the project?"

They agreed to meet the day after next, and she gave Cassie her address. Aerin hung up feeling a little better about fulfilling her destiny. The day was crisp and clear, and she continued her walk to a nearby park she'd last been to years ago. The cool breeze carried the scent of dying leaves, and Aerin relished every breath. This time last year, she was finishing her internship for her MSW. She'd just slept with a woman for the first time in ages. She was pulling away from Josh, spending more time out of the house, more nights at Zoe's and on weekend trips she'd taken by herself.

In the year since, everything had changed in the best possible way. For a brief moment, it was perfect. She had the person she longed for, and they were taking care of an awesome kid. She still had trouble believing it was all over. Now, her life looked mostly the same as it had right after her divorce. Alone except for Zoe, bound to a path she hadn't chosen, and wishing for something else. Wishing for Olivia back in her life.

As if a divine presence had heard her thoughts, she looked up to see Olivia heading toward her, carrying a to-go cup. Olivia didn't notice her, and she walked with her head down. Her gait no longer exuded confidence like it had. It was the gait of a broken woman. Aerin stopped her forward motion, frozen between turning around and running away and yelling out for her. Olivia looked up to avoid a collision and did a double take. They stood in front of one another in shocked silence. Aerin studied her face as she struggled with her own words. What could she say? Olivia's cheeks shone with what appeared to be embarrassment, regret, disappointment. Aerin felt the same.

Suddenly, they were hugging, Olivia's arms around her, squeezing her as if when she let go, Aerin would disappear forever. It wasn't all joy, though. It was desperation and uncertainty. Aerin could feel it deep down in the bottom of Olivia's mind, almost forgotten but sure to unearth itself in a moment of trial.

"Hi," Aerin said against Olivia's shoulder.

"Hi."

They broke apart and stood at arm's length, studying each other. Olivia had on a dark-blue scarf in addition to her usual gray suit jacket. Instead of her usual matching pants, she wore jeans that hugged her slender form.

"How's Evie?"

Olivia shrugged. "She's okay. I got her a dog. Doing well in school." Near the end, she trailed off, and her eyes grew sad.

"Maybe she could come over soon and visit."

Olivia nodded. "She'd like that. Um, how are you?"

"I'm doing fine." When Aerin didn't elaborate or ask her how she was doing, Olivia shifted from one foot to the other.

"I'm sorry about the museum," she said after an eternity.

Too little, too late, Aerin thought, though she knew she was being cruel. Her insides were beginning to knot up, and she was starting to feel ill. She didn't like whatever this was between them. It wasn't right, toeing the line between elation and despair. "Okay, well, have Evie text me when she wants to come visit. Nice seeing you."

With that, Aerin left Olivia staring at the ground. Halfway down the block, she allowed herself one tear, for nostalgia's sake.

CHAPTER THIRTY-FOUR

It turned out Evie was so eager to come over, they arranged for that to happen the very next day. Aerin put out cheese and crackers for Evie's first visit to her new apartment. She straightened the pillows on the couch and hoped it looked as appealing as Olivia's place. She wanted Evie to consider it a second home.

"It feels weird for you not to be there when I get home every day," Evie said. She was sitting on Aerin's couch, feet up on the coffee table, drinking soda from a coffee mug.

"I know, honey. I wish things were different."

Evie perked up at her admission. "Really? Olivia wants you to come back."

Something surged in Aerin's chest, and she had to take a sip of tea before she could speak again. "Olivia will come around in her own time, or she won't. Either way, I'd love to have you over whenever you want."

Evie nodded and sank back into the cushions. "Are you dating somebody else?"

Aerin thought about the hardware-store clerk and blushed, even though she'd never said more than two sentences to them. "No. Olivia and I love each other, but sometimes things are more complicated than that."

"You haven't even met Marsha yet," Evie said.

"Want to show me some pictures?"

Evie scooted over and took out her phone. She seemed happier when she was focused on the dog. Good job, Olivia, for getting her one. In fact, Evie had all but forgotten about questioning their relationship when she scrolled to a picture taken at Pride. The three of them grinned into the sunlight as Olivia reached her long arm out and took the selfie.

"I know you're not my real parents, but it was better when you were both there."

Despite a little voice warning her against it, Aerin asked the question that had been on her mind for the past couple of weeks. "How's she doing?" She hadn't exactly found out anything of substance when she ran into her yesterday.

"She's sad. I think she maybe tried to call you a few times but didn't know what to say."

She should have, Aerin thought. She always told her clients it was never too late to apologize, but that was a lie. There was a point of no return. She got the hint. Olivia didn't want complicated, and that was all Aerin had to offer. Aerin wasn't going to become someone else any time soon, and Olivia wasn't going to change her mind. It was pure stubbornness, as far as she could tell. An inability to accept that Aerin wasn't the same as she had been.

Despite everything, Aerin did want Olivia to come around. It was going to take more than a halfhearted apology on the street. Though she was still figuring out how to see into the future, she had a nagging feeling that things weren't over between them.

"Anyway, how's your new job?" Evie asked.

"Really stressful but good to have a paycheck. How's school?"

"Good. I have a lot more classes to choose from here, so I'm taking an AP Physics class that Tameka's in, too." Evie got a funny look on her face when she mentioned Tameka.

"Oh? So are you two good friends now?"

Evie averted her eyes. "Uh-huh. We had a sleepover the other night."

Aerin waited for more details, but Evie didn't volunteer any. "What did you two do? Watch movies? Make prank calls? Summon some spirits in the bathroom mirror?"

Evie was on the verge of laughter. "Are those things you used to do? Summon spirits? How do you even make a prank call? You can tell who's calling."

"All right, all right. Different times, my friend. So?"

"We went for a walk."

"Sounds fun."

"And she kissed me."

"Um, what? Out of nowhere?"

"Oh, no. She asked me if I'd ever kissed a girl. I told her I wanted to. And don't tell Olivia because she might not let me sleep over anymore."

It was Aerin's turn to laugh. "I don't think Olivia has any intention of preventing that from happening. That's the same age we were when we started dating. She knows how it is."

Evie's eyes grew wide. "Oh."

"Yeah. I think you'll find she's a good person to talk to about that." She was usually a good person to talk to about lots of things, but Aerin couldn't verify if that was still true.

Evie nodded, seeming to consider the suggestion.

Aerin remembered her role as a very part-time parent, if you could even call it that anymore. "That's great, though, your first kiss?" She took Evie's hands and squeezed them.

"You don't have to make such a big deal out of it," Evie said, wriggling away. "It's just a kiss."

"There's the teenager we rarely get to see." They both noticed her use of "we," and thankfully, Evie didn't bring it up.

"I have to jump in the shower really quickly. Why don't you choose a restaurant you want to go to?"

Evie picked up her phone and started typing something in. "Can it be fancy?"

Aerin stopped in the doorway of the bathroom and smiled, relishing being able to give the answer she wanted to, now that she had a steady job with enough income to splurge every once in a while. "As fancy as you want."

She left Evie to choose what would likely be the most expensive restaurant she could find and shut herself in the bathroom. She loved this kid, but her visit sure brought up some thoughts and feelings Aerin had been working hard to suppress.

As she stepped out of the shower, she heard a crash. "Evie? Everything okay?"

A muffled voice answered. "What is this thing?"

Oh, shit. Evie had gone into her guest room, which she'd failed to tell her was very much off-limits due to the secret project she was trying to carry out. She threw on a T-shirt and jeans and ran out to make sure Evie hadn't gone too far in. Though she hadn't accumulated many parts yet, the room was a mess with tools and tacked-up plans.

"Hey, actually that room is off-limits."

"Well, what is it? What is all this stuff?"

Aerin was frozen between telling her a white lie that would surely come back to bite her in the ass or actually divulging the truth. The truth might tax her credibility with Evie and give her too much of an insight into her struggle with Olivia.

Evie crossed her arms and stood in the middle of the room wide-legged. "Are you building a bomb?"

"No. I'm not building a bomb." Aerin hadn't really considered what she was building definitely looked like a bomb. She didn't want Evie running to the cops or even to Olivia. She had only one choice. She had to tell her the truth. "Maybe the restaurant can wait. We should talk in private."

She could see Evie's pupils dilate, a sure sign she was nervous about what she was about to hear. She had good instincts. It wasn't going to be pretty.

"Here, sit next to me. Settle in. It's going to be a long story." Aerin drew her knees to her chest and leaned sideways against the cushions on the back of the couch. She grabbed a periwinkle throw pillow and squeezed it rhythmically with her fingers, hoping that after this, Evie would still trust her. God knows she'd bet wrong against Olivia.

"Are you going to start?"

Aerin's hesitation was making both of them more anxious. "Yeah. I am. I just want you to know this is going to sound very weird and that I'm not making any of it up."

"Okay."

"Evie, I'm not sure if you're aware of the debate about multiple universes and how they may or may not be connected to ours."

"A little."

"Well, they exist, and one of them is connected to our universe through a portal in the bottom of a lake in upstate New York." Aerin took a deep breath. She could hear the pounding rock music in the apartment below her and the traffic going by on her busy street and the water rushing through pipes in the bathroom from her upstairs neighbor. She focused on anything she could to take her mind off Evie's reaction.

"I believe you."

Aerin looked into Evie's eyes. They were kind, devoid of judgment. "You do?"

"Tameka told me stories about stuff like that. She thinks it's just stories that her uncle made up, but I'm certain you're telling the truth."

Aerin nodded, still shocked that Evie had believed her so easily, really believed her, not because Aerin had convinced her to.

"Is there more?"

So much more. "Long story short, I went on vacation last April and when I was in a lake, I was infected by energy from another universe. Alien energy."

"Rhunan?"

"How did you know?"

"Tameka's uncle tells her about them all the time and how they'll make the world a better place when they get here. She thinks it's just to scare her into being a good person or something." Evie picked up her half-full mug of soda, sipped, and made a face. "Too warm."

"You can get more."

"It's okay. I'll order some at the fancy restaurant we're going to."

Aerin's heart warmed. She hadn't even blinked. Olivia's reaction seemed even more outsized now.

"Does Olivia know about the alien inside you?"

Aerin shifted on the couch so that both her feet were on the floor. "Unfortunately, yes. She helped me figure out what was going on, but she would rather I didn't have it."

Evie shrugged. "If it's not hurting you and it's not hurting her, why does she care?"

"She doesn't know if her feelings for me are real or if I manipulated her with the alien powers."

"But haven't you guys been in love since you were my age?"

"Well, yeah."

"So what's the problem?"

"That's the question, isn't it?"

"I'll convince her."

Aerin shook her head and laughed halfheartedly. "You don't really have to do that, honey."

"I want to. I liked it better when you were together."

"Thanks. Well, I can't condone it, but if you do say something, just don't let her think it was my idea."

Evie nodded and drummed her fingers on the arm of the couch. "Someone's getting hungry," Aerin said.

"Yeah. Let's go."

"Okay, but first, do you have any more questions for me?"

"No. I'm ready to eat."

Aerin rose from the couch and held out her hand to hoist Evie up. She gathered her keys and a light jacket. "You going to put the directions in your phone and navigate for me?"

"Yup."

By the time they were finally on the road and Evie was guaranteed a forthcoming meal, she became curious again.

"Tell me about all those pieces of sheet metal in that room."

"I thought you were done asking questions."

"Nope. You were just being too slow."

Aerin sighed and chuckled. "Okay. I'll tell you all about the stuff in that room if you promise not to bring it up in front of other people. Deal?" Aerin stuck out her hand for Evie to shake.

"Deal," Evie said, her warm hand in Aerin's.

The next morning, Evie had just left for school when Aerin's doorbell rang. It took her a moment to remember that she'd set an appointment with Cassie to go over her project, so she didn't answer until the second ring.

"I'm going to buzz you up," she said into the intercom. "Third floor, third apartment on the left."

"Got it," Cassie said. That voice. She'd definitely heard it somewhere before.

While she wracked her brain to place it, Cassie knocked at her door. Opening it answered her question immediately. Before her stood the clerk from the hardware store. Aerin blushed at the sight of Cassie in their work overalls, leaning against the door frame with an easiness they must have worked hard to cultivate. Cassie also looked surprised to see her.

"Oh, hi," they said.

"Uh, hi. Nice to see you again. I'm Aerin." She held out her hand and almost melted at Cassie's firm grip. Maybe hiring them wasn't such a great idea.

"Brought my tool belt out of habit, but don't mind me. I know this isn't one of those calls," Cassie said with a smirk.

"Never know when something around here might break."

"Oh? One of those absentee landlords?"

Not at all, Aerin thought, but she'd started it, so she had to continue. "Heh. Yup. Anyway, have a seat at the kitchen table."

She poured them both glasses of water and placed the list in front of Cassie. "These are all the components I have to get."

Cassie leaned their elbows on the table and placed their chin in their hands. "Quite a list you have here."

"I know. How long will it take you to find all that stuff?"

"Not too long. I know a lot of people in a lot of places. Half of this we have at the hardware store."

Aerin exhaled forcefully. "Great. You're hired, but only for five hours a week. I can't really afford more than that."

"What if I get it all done sooner, and you pay me in installments?"

Cute and smart. "Deal." They shook on it, Cassie's eyes appraising Aerin from head to torso.

"I'll get started later today and text you an update," Cassie said.

Aerin walked Cassie out and stood against the closed door for a moment to collect herself. Cassie made her heart flutter, but it was just a temporary infatuation. Nothing like the depth of feeling she grudgingly still had for Olivia.

CHAPTER THIRTY-FIVE

Olivia parked her car in the faculty lot and glanced at the bouquet of roses in the backseat. They seemed like such an absurd gesture, slightly wilted and bought at a gas station. Screw it. They were better than nothing. She got out of the car and grabbed them, then slammed the door. She'd wasted three weeks already. Seeing Aerin two days ago had awakened feelings that didn't care whether Aerin was 100 percent human or 100 percent jungle cat.

Evie had been more than willing to give her Aerin's address on her way to school, which made Olivia wonder what they'd discussed. It didn't matter. Aerin had been right. She was choosing to be obtuse about their situation. Nothing had changed since they'd reconnected, and she'd been slowly falling back in love with Aerin since then. There was everything else, too—all the messages from Murray and that woman and the cryptic fire that seemed to unearth Max's notes. She had two choices: ignore all the signs and keep being a stubborn ass, or admit she was wrong. The second option didn't come easy for her.

She ambled toward Aerin's apartment, hoping it was early enough that Aerin would still be at home getting ready for work. As she neared the building, her heart began to pound, and her palms sweated against the plastic wrapping the flowers. This was a busy section of street on a weekday morning, and Olivia wondered how Aerin enjoyed living in such a bustling area after spending a lifetime in Tireville. She'd find out soon enough.

Someone was coming out the front door as she got there, and she caught it before she was locked out. This would work much better if Aerin didn't have the chance to turn her away before hearing what she had to say. As she rounded the corner to Aerin's apartment, she heard voices. Someone had just left. Hiding behind a corner, she watched an attractive queer person with a smug smile saunter out of the building. She could come up with only one reason someone would leave another person's apartment in the morning. And with Evie over, too? Shit. It must be serious between them. She was too late.

Devastated, Olivia tossed the flowers into a garbage can outside the building and began the long walk back to campus. The last thing she wanted to see when she returned to her office was the large box from Max containing Murray's unburned papers. It reminded her too much of why she'd lost Aerin this time. Her friend and colleague Jody stopped by just as Olivia was standing over the box, contemplating whether she wanted to see what was inside.

"Hey, partner. How you holding up?"

"Okay, I guess."

"That good?" Jody squeezed Olivia's shoulder.

Olivia didn't want to share her embarrassing morning, but Jody was giving her such a sincere look, she couldn't help it. "I tried to go apologize, but Aerin's dating someone new."

"So soon?"

Olivia shrugged and sat on her desk next to the box. "She's a catch. Are you really so surprised?"

"Hm. What's in that box?"

"Papers from that researcher in Canada who first wrote about that guy Murray I told you about. The one who was also infected with alien energy from the lake."

Jody took out her keys and flipped the blade of a small Swiss Army knife. "Well? What are you waiting for?"

"I guess I was waiting for someone to come along with an illicit keychain knife."

Jody sliced open the top and sides. Max hadn't taped it shut very well, and the tape had almost come off one flap. He'd clearly thrown the papers in there and then sent them out as quickly as he could.

Within the packing material, a large rubber band held together two bundles of yellowing paper. Max must have kept it in an attic or crawl space because it smelled slightly musty. The rubber bands had deep cracks and disintegrated as soon as Jody lifted the bundles out.

"You'll have a lot to read tonight," Jody said.

"Good thing, because I don't have anything else to do."

"Oh, honey, you mean anyone else. I'm sure you have lots you can do with Evie or Mr. Piddles or that dog of yours. You could catch up on *Sunrise Lane.*"

Olivia sighed and leaned into Jody's arm. "You're right."

"I know. I'm your fairy gaymother."

She chuckled. "I think that means you would be the gay one, not me."

"Shush. I was just on my way to a faculty meeting. Why don't we catch up later before you have to go home?"

"Yeah," Olivia said. Her voice fried out, eliciting a look of concern from Jody as she headed out into the hallway.

She wanted nothing to do with Murray and Max's papers, but they were here in front of her, and she couldn't exactly stick them back in the mail and return them. There had to be some reason the fire had left these untouched.

Olivia flipped quickly through the piles of notebook and computer paper, printed and inked by hand. Some of it was in Murray's writing, and some of it must have been Max's interview notes. She sighed. Today had gone to hell in a handbasket. Then, as though someone were looking out for her from above, her office phone rang.

"Hello?"

"Mrs. Ando? This is Abby Stone, the principal at East Indianapolis High. We need you to come down here immediately."

Olivia was only too happy to comply. "Of course. I'll be there in fifteen minutes."

Evie's school was a monstrous brick building that had been built a hundred years ago and periodically expanded. The bright-red bricks of the wings clashed with the seasoned maroon of the rest of the building. The inside hadn't been updated since the seventies. The security officer waved her through to the principal's office. When Olivia arrived at the door, she saw Evie through the glass.

She immediately sat down next to Evie and drew her close. "Hey, what happened?"

Evie sniffled. "This guy was making fun of my accent, so I punched him."

"Oh?"

"He told me to go back to whatever shithole country I came from."

"Good for you," Olivia said.

Evie snapped her head up. "Huh?"

"You heard me. He deserved it. Did he get in trouble, too?"

"They told him not to say stuff like that and then sent him back to class. They're giving me a week of in-school suspension because of the zero-tolerance policy."

Olivia scoffed. "Zero tolerance for what?"

"Violence."

"Oh, fuck that. I'll be right back."

She left Evie in the chair and stormed into the principal's office. Principal Stone was on the phone with someone, though she hung up quickly when she saw Olivia's looming, angry figure.

"Mrs. Ando, have a seat," she said.

"First of all, it's Ms. Ando or Mx. Ando, and second, Evie will not be serving any kind of punishment for responding appropriately to a little Nazi wannabe who thinks he can intimidate women because his fragile masculinity cannot fathom a world in which he is not in power." She took a deep breath and sat in one of the chairs.

Principal Stone's eyebrows seemed to be stuck in the raised position. "Well, thank you for that impassioned speech. We do have a no-tolerance violence policy in this school that speaks pretty clearly on the matter."

"Well, Ms. Stone, then it is imperative that the school change its policy to include hate speech, which is a form of violence. If you'd like, I would be happy to put together a bibliography of studies that prove it has the same effects. I'd certainly be willing to share it with the school board or a national news station as well. You know I have a lot of media connections, right? I'm the one they call when they want to do a popular-science segment on the brain."

Principal Stone gulped, stared at her for a moment, and then picked up the phone, poised to dial. "I'll consult with the vice principal. He handles disciplinary procedures, and I'm sure he'd be willing to give Evie a day of suspension instead of a week."

Olivia sat a little taller and grinned placidly. "That would be great. And while you're at it, I'd suggest mandatory counseling for the young man who seems to think it's okay to be a white supremacist."

"Send him to counseling? I don't think—"

"I don't care what you think. You messed up by letting him off the hook, and you'll make it better. What Evie did was no worse than what he did, and I hope you'll be sending him home as well. I will not let that girl suffer alone because of your small-mindedness."

Principal Stone sighed. "I'll discuss it with the vice principal. And I'll suggest counseling to his parents."

"Good. I'm going to go now and take Evie with me. She'll come back to school tomorrow and be greeted with a sincere apology from that young man. And we'll put this whole thing behind us."

Principal Stone made a few notes on her notepad. "It was a pleasure meeting you, Ms. Ando."

"Likewise." Olivia stood shook Principal Stone's hand, then exited the office.

"Come on. Let's get out of here," she said to Evie.

"They're letting me leave?"

She laughed. "They're making you leave, but you'll be back tomorrow. Don't expect any more trouble from that kid. Look, I'm proud of you for standing up for yourself, but next time, maybe try a different angle, okay? No punching. Gather evidence, take your case to the principal, and if that doesn't work, I'll help you take it to the school board. No violence from you. Ben can tell you all about how people will treat you differently than your white classmates when you do something like this. It's not your fault, and it's not fair, but it's real. Okay?"

"Yeah. Sorry."

Olivia took Evie's hands and lifted her from the chair. "Want to take boxing lessons? There's a gym on my way to work that offers them. I'll even go with you."

Evie looked at her in disbelief. "Are you for real?"

Olivia put a hand on the back of Evie's neck and squeezed. "I've never been more serious in my life."

CHAPTER THIRTY-SIX

Without Aerin to share some of the workload, Olivia found herself on more frequent drives from Indianapolis to Tireville. Emmanuel and Evie wanted to see each other every weekend and some weeknights, but Olivia had a thousand excuses to keep their trips to a minimum. Today she didn't have one, and Mariko had found a three-hour block of time when Martin would be out of the house. She really couldn't say no.

Marsha sat in Evie's lap the whole way to Olivia's childhood home. She regarded it now with curiosity rather than familiarity. The house and grounds were way too formal for her, and the thought she'd once lived here was bizarre. It did, however, highlight where she'd learned some of her less-attractive habits regarding excessive cleanliness.

She and Evie arrived in the early afternoon to a freshly cooked lunch of rice, chicken, and vegetables with a mouthwatering ginger sauce—the food of Olivia's childhood. Emmanuel waited until the exact time when Olivia and Evie took plates to fill his with food.

"Emmanuel, stop being so greedy. I told you to wait until they took their food," Mariko said.

"You said to wait until they got here."

"Put it down until everyone has some."

Emmanuel hung his head and slid his plate onto the table. "Okay."

"Mom, it's fine. Emmanuel, you can eat whenever you're ready," said Olivia. Mariko passed her a stern look.

"You think because you're taking care of Evie now that you can make the rules in this house?"

She sheepishly looked to Emmanuel for support, but he had averted his gaze. He knew where this path led. They were both Mariko's children, and they both had to respect Mariko's rules, no matter how much they'd grown.

"Sorry," Olivia said. Emmanuel echoed her a moment later. Mariko nodded and filled a plate for herself as if no argument had occurred. She'd always had that power to let go of her feelings and move on as if nothing had happened.

"So, tell me, Evie, are you doing well in school?"

Evie nodded and glanced at Olivia, who gave her a small head shake. Mariko would freak out if she found out about Evie's punching incident. She was better off neglecting to mention it.

"And this dog of yours? Well-behaved?"

Evie looked down at Marsha, who was curled in a ball at her feet. She seemed to know when to be on her best behavior and when she could get away with tearing around the house on a toy-hunting spree. "She's sleeping right now. She listens to me. Olivia taught me how she trained Mr. Piddles, and I've been doing that with Marsha."

"Good. You two finish up and go upstairs to play," Mariko said to the kids.

This was the part Olivia dreaded: having to make small talk with her mother. They'd found more and more to discuss lately, but conversation never flowed too easily. They always left something unsaid, some words unspoken.

Once the kids went upstairs, Mariko gestured Olivia to the couch.

"What about the dishes?" Olivia asked.

"I'll deal with them later."

This was new. Olivia remembered her mother making sure the house was spotless at all times, and that included doing the dishes right after each meal. Martin didn't like it when things weren't clean.

"What's up?" Her mother was fidgeting with her hands and tapping her foot, more frazzled than Olivia had ever seen her.

"I'm going to need your help in about a week."

Olivia's skin prickled and her hackles went up. Her mother asking her for help again? She shuddered at what it could be this time.

"I'm leaving your father and taking Emmanuel with me. It won't be easy, but I'm done."

"Holy fuck." That was all Olivia could say.

"Language."

"Um, what's going on?"

"He's going to find out about the program I'm running, and he won't be happy."

"Program?"

Mariko sighed. "Evie isn't the first or the last child we've moved from dangerous fundamentalist households."

Whoa. So many questions. Olivia leaned back in her armchair and wiped her hand over her mouth. "Who's 'we'?"

"I can't tell you exactly who, but we have a group of mostly spouses or adult children of fundamentalist religious leaders. We relocate gay and lesbian and transgender children who are in danger, with the help of people who are very good at persuasion. Evie was one of the children. That's not the point of what I'm trying to tell you, though."

"Uh." People good at persuasion? That phrase sounded oddly familiar.

"I need your help. I will have a small window to get my things and disappear without him knowing. And Emmanuel is coming with me. We need to stay with you for a night or two until we can find somewhere safe to live." Mariko spoke without emotion, as if she were simply making plans for a weekend trip, not about to uproot her entire life and leave her abusive husband.

"I mean, yeah, I'll help you, but can we go back to the thing with the kids? How big is this network? Is this legal?"

"Olivia, pay attention to what's important here. We can count on you to come by? What about Aerin? Can she come, too?"

Olivia's mouth went dry at the mention of her now double-ex-girlfriend. "Um, we're not really together anymore."

"What?" Mariko shouted. She obviously realized how loud she was being and immediately toned it down. "What happened to you two? I thought you would finally settle down."

"So did I."

"What did you do?"

Olivia threw her hands in the air. "Why do you assume I did something to mess it up?"

"Did you?"

"I guess."

"Well?"

She huffed. "Fine. I told her I didn't like something about her she can't change."

"So you just walked away?"

"She also lied to me," Olivia said defensively.

"Did she lie or omit information?"

God damn, that woman had a spooky knack for getting to the bottom of Olivia's bullshit. "She didn't tell me something, and I took it personally."

"Have you ever not told her something?"

"Probably." Lots of times, Olivia thought.

"Well, go apologize to her."

"She's seeing someone else now. I was planning to apologize, but I saw this other person leave her apartment."

"So you're just going to give up."

Olivia didn't have a rebuttal. She *was* just going to give up. It didn't make sense, but then neither did chasing a person who was through with her. Whether Aerin had actually made that clear or Olivia had just assumed wasn't the point. She couldn't go back.

Olivia shifted in her seat. She wasn't in the mood for an interrogation today, so she changed the subject. "Aerin won't be there to help you unless you ask her yourself."

"Okay. I'll ask her. But I'm disappointed it's ended between the two of you."

"Yeah, well, so am I."

Mariko continued to give Olivia questioning looks until she excused herself to go check on the kids. As she expected, they were upstairs playing with Marsha.

"Watch this new trick we taught her," Emmanuel exclaimed when Olivia entered the room.

Evie clapped twice, and Marsha rolled over twice in a row.

"Have you tried three claps yet?" Olivia asked.

Evie and Emmanuel looked at each other with wide eyes. "No. We just got two."

"See if she's responding to that particular command or if she associates one clap with one roll."

Evie clapped her hands three times, and Marsha whimpered. "She doesn't know what to do."

Olivia knelt in front of Marsha and looked into her eyes. They seemed to show intelligence that went beyond doing simple tricks for treats, but it was probably an evolutionary adaptation to fool humans into doing anything for her. Either way, she would get this with a little practice. "Try again slowly, from one clap per roll."

Evie clapped and Marsha rolled. She clapped and she rolled again. Soon they were in a rhythm of clapping and rolling that took Marsha across the wide room.

"Now two."

Evie resumed her clapping, and Marsha did as she'd been taught.

"Try three again."

This time, when Evie clapped three times, Marsha rolled over the same number.

"Wow," Evie said. Emmanuel whooped and hollered as Olivia high-fived them.

"Now that is the power of scientific inquiry."

"Olivia," Mariko called from downstairs.

"Yeah?"

"Can you come down here, please?"

She made an involuntary teenageresque groaning noise, which earned her incredulous looks from the actual teenagers in the room. "Oh, please. You both would have the same reaction."

Downstairs, Mariko was tapping the silver cordless phone against her palm. "Aerin isn't dating anybody."

"I'm sorry?"

"Aerin is single and waiting for you to apologize. Meg confirmed it. Just thought you would want to know so you can go fix things."

Olivia squeezed her eyes shut and shook her head. Was her semi-estranged mother really butting into her love life?

"You're welcome." Mariko raised an eyebrow.

Olivia wouldn't fall for it. "Is it almost time for us to go?"

Mariko sighed and shuddered slightly, it seemed. "Yes, unfortunately."

"Text me with the details of what you'll need for your great escape."

"Don't be crass. Thank you for your help."

Olivia wanted to thank Mariko for somehow being involved in a top-secret operation to save kids from their dangerous families, but she was too miffed about her mother's assessment of her relationship. Petty, but when it came to being her mother's daughter, some things would never change.

CHAPTER THIRTY-SEVEN

Today was a day of reckoning. Olivia had seen many of them in her years at the church, but today was the first time she'd felt the judgment against her: that visceral weight on her heart that refused to budge and could only be remedied by confessing all her sins. She ate a hearty breakfast with Evie before school, then dressed in her best gray suit and headed out the door.

Evie had relayed Aerin's typical work schedule, and today it sounded like she'd be home early. Olivia hoped that assumption was true, because two failed attempts at reconciliation would seem like some kind of sign. She met with a few students during office hours, going over assignments they'd misunderstood or under-researched, before teaching a class of freshmen. Neuroscience 101 wasn't her favorite course, but it brought in numbers to her department, and most of the students hadn't been jaded by college yet. After letting them out half an hour early, she closed herself in her office and mentally rehearsed her speech.

Aerin, I was reckless. Aerin, let me make it up to you, please. Aerin, you are everything to me, and I truly don't care if you're an alien or cyborg or dinosaur. Maybe that wasn't necessarily true, but she'd get the sentiment.

Sweating heavily underneath the thick wool of her suit, Olivia made her way to Aerin's apartment. It was fifteen minutes away on foot, and she quickly began to regret her clothing choices, even though the suit made her look extra sharp. As she walked, she clenched and unclenched her jaw, imagining all the different scenarios for how her apology might play out. After she said and did everything possible, she'd be leaving with either a second chance or no chance. As the apartment building came into view, she took a deep breath. Aerin's car was in the parking lot of the small complex. At least she'd be getting some kind of answer today.

This time she took a chance and rang the doorbell, hoping Aerin would buzz her up when she realized who was at the door.

"Hello?" Aerin asked over the intercom.

"Uh, hi. It's me. Olivia. Can we talk?" Her voice shook, and so did her hands, as she wrung them in front of her.

After a brief pause that Olivia's heart mimicked, a low tone indicated the door was open. She walked inside, conscious of each step as she drew closer to Aerin's apartment and the answers that lay within. A lovely fall wreath hung from the door, and Olivia found herself longing to cozy up with Aerin as the leaves fell outside, sipping hot tea and watching movies. Before Olivia could knock, the door opened. Aerin's face was tight, her brows knitted together over unyielding eyes.

"You can come in," Aerin said.

It occurred to Olivia that they'd arrived full circle in just a few short months. Back then, she'd been the reluctant homeowner on the other side of the door, and in some cruel twist, history seemed doomed to repeat itself. She stepped through the door, feeling awkward about being there for the first time under these circumstances. Aerin's apartment was cluttered in a way that made it feel inhabited, and Olivia immediately wanted to stay there forever. She looked around and saw the same pieces of furniture that Aerin had used at her old house. Olivia still had the La-Z-Boy and a few of Aerin's other possessions, but the bulk of her decor was here. She was about to comment on how nice it had turned out, when she heard a loud clang coming from behind a closed door.

"Everything okay in there, Cassie?" Aerin shouted.

Cassie? Was that the person she saw coming from Aerin's the other day? Suddenly, things were less clear—Aerin's availability and Olivia's ability to speak.

Aerin immediately noticed Olivia's discomfort and sighed. "Cassie is helping me with the machine."

"Ah."

"So?" Aerin folded her arms and waited.

Olivia couldn't see herself having this conversation with someone else so close by. "Do you want to get out of here?"

Aerin shrugged and grabbed a light jacket. "Where are we going?"

Olivia thought quickly about places that might be deserted at this hour and came up empty, so Aerin decided for them. "There's a cemetery not too far away. Crown Hill. We probably wouldn't run into anyone."

Olivia nodded and led Aerin out of the building. After they'd walked in silence for too long, she gathered the courage to speak. "I'm sorry. I was an ass." It came out as a cross between a mutter and a croak.

"What?" Aerin asked.

"I said I'm sorry. For what I said."

"I heard the word 'ass' in there somewhere," Aerin said.

Olivia smacked her lightly on the arm. "Fine. I deserved that. Anyway, I don't know why I was so obsessed with how you got to be the way you are, because I love that person."

"Interesting way of showing it."

Olivia's gut churned with regret. "I assume you mean the long silence?"

Aerin kept her eyes on the sidewalk. They passed a couple walking a dog and pushing a stroller. Olivia noticed how Aerin followed them with her gaze until they were out of view.

"I tried to apologize the night after Evie slept over, but Callie, or whatever that person's name is, was coming out of your apartment. I thought you were dating her."

"Them."

"Huh?"

"Cassie is their name, and they use 'they' pronouns."

"Oh, right. Anyway, that's the only reason I put this off so long," Olivia said.

"That and the fact that you still hadn't accepted who I am now?" Aerin gave her a challenging look.

"That's not entirely true. Maybe a little. You know me. I get caught on an idea, and I can't let it go. Look at that ridiculous project I've been working on for years—a program that would decipher emotional intentions even if the subject wasn't aware of what they were? You have to admit that's ludicrous."

"You're pretty stubborn."

"Evie might have made some good points like that at dinner the other night. So did some other people, including my mom." Olivia cringed at the memory of her mother checking up on Aerin through Meg. In the end, she was glad for the information, but they weren't in high school anymore. Mother-to-mother phone calls shouldn't be part of being in an adult relationship.

"Yeah. Mom told me Mariko called and asked if I was dating somebody. She thought it was very strange."

"It was. I let my mother know as much."

They'd reached the entrance to the cemetery and stepped inside. Olivia wasn't sure whether she should have agreed to put everything on the line here, especially when some of these people might have died for doing the same.

"Let's go this way." She pointed to the right, and they set off on one of the many meandering paths. If they didn't get lost here, it would be a miracle.

"Why did you come to my apartment today? What do you want from me?"

"I want to start over."

Aerin scoffed. "Sorry? I don't think we can just start over. It doesn't work like that. Lots of water under this bridge."

"I know. Maybe what I mean is that we can start over with the understanding that we're different people now than we were, but we still love each other. I mean, if that's the way you feel."

Aerin nodded noncommittally. "We'll see. You can start by telling me everything you've kept from me."

"Deal." They continued walking.

"You can start any time."

"Right. Okay, well, I've had a lot of dreams of another world in the connected universe. Murray was in one of them. He told me I should help you. And that lady at Pride, she told me the same."

"That person who bumped into you?" Aerin asked.

"That was her. Came out of nowhere, ended up across the street, and then disappeared."

"Someone was trying to send you a message."

"Loud and clear. I was ignoring it because I just really wanted to be in a normal relationship."

"I suppose I understand where you're coming from. Trust me, I'd love to not have this thing in my head anymore. Life was so much simpler before I went to the lake."

"Which time?" Olivia asked. They laughed, and the sound faded into awkward silence.

Aerin opened her mouth like she was about to say something. Olivia gave her an encouraging nod.

"I guess it's only fair if I share, too. You should know that I helped your mom with Evie's parents. It was actually really easy for them to give her up, which is terrible."

Olivia was relieved to know she'd been right. "I had a feeling you had something to do with that."

"I feel awful about it in some ways, but Evie's doing really well here. She would have suffered under her parents. By the time we extracted her, she was already suffering."

Olivia understood. Lately, she was coming around to the idea that her mother had done her a favor by sending her to Chicago.

"Thank you," she said. She stopped walking and turned to Aerin, taking one of her hands. "I am so, so sorry about what happened between us. I don't know what I was thinking. You're amazing, and you deserve someone who will love you no matter what powers you do or do not have." She took a deep breath. "That person is me, if you'll have me back."

Aerin demurred. "I'm doing my best to figure out my powers, but they still exist. What you see is what you get."

"I know."

Aerin smiled a little and took her hand back. "I think we have more to discuss."

It wasn't a "no." She'd take it. They began walking again. "I have some papers I need to share with you. Max sent them. He's the researcher who wrote the original paper we found about Murray."

"What do they say?"

"That's about as important as how I got them. It seems like they were uncovered for us. There was a fire in Max's office, and the only surviving objects were these papers. Totally untouched. He'd forgotten he had them."

"Hm. Are you going to tell me what's in them?" Aerin asked.

"It's the whole story from Murray's childhood to the 80s. His life. What he'd seen. The part that concerns you, though, is where he told Max that he's going to deeply regret a decision he's going to make in the future. Max asks him what he's talking about, and he says he doesn't know yet."

"He hadn't had the dream about the machine yet."

"I suppose not. You'll have to read it yourself to understand better. It doesn't make much sense to me."

Aerin glanced at her. "You didn't happen to bring it with you, did you?"

Damn. That would have been a much better gift than the flowers she'd brought and dumped on her aborted visit. She shook her head.

"Tell you what. We kind of rushed into things last time. We should have spent more time on our own, but that didn't even occur to me until after I left. We've kept things from one another, and even though we both communicate for a living, we seem to suck at it in our personal lives," said Aerin.

"Agreed."

"What if we agree to take it really slowly, actually date this time? Otherwise I have a feeling we might end up in the museum again, surrounded by dead body parts, breaking up."

Olivia's spirit was buoyant. "I promise to help you do anything you need with this machine of yours."

Aerin took her hand and squeezed it. Funny how such a small gesture made her entire world feel right again. "Cassie's been a great help, actually. I'm not too far away from being done, though I'm going to be out thousands of dollars. But I'm not asking you for financial help or anything," she said.

"You just let me know what you need."

Aerin nodded. "I was hoping you'd come around on the whole alien thing. Mom told me I was wasting my time, but I knew you would."

"Well, you can see the future, after all."

Aerin scrunched her brow. "Things have changed a bit. The explosion in the lake fused the Rhunan energy with my consciousness. I can't seem to manipulate it anymore. Things come in bits and pieces, but I'm not in control."

"I'm sure you'll learn how to control it again," Olivia said.

"You sure you want that?"

"Hey, it makes you that much more interesting than you already were."

"Gee, thanks," Aerin said, elbowing Olivia as they walked.

"I didn't mean—"

"I know." Aerin twisted Olivia around so they faced each other and moved in so their noses were almost touching. Olivia could feel her warm breath and see tiny droplets of sweat on her upper lip. She turned her head just so and brought their lips together. It was everything she'd been missing, the heat and familiarity, the way Aerin's tongue always made its way past Olivia's parted lips.

"Maybe you want to sleep over tonight?" Olivia asked hopefully.

Aerin bit her bottom lip. "We should probably take things slower than that."

"Right. I forgot."

"Short-term memory problems, and so young." Aerin smirked.

They walked hand in hand back to Aerin's apartment so she could check on Cassie.

Before they parted ways, Olivia realized she had one more piece of news. "I totally forgot. My mom and Emmanuel are coming to live with me. She's leaving Martin. She wants you to help spring them out of the house, if you can."

"She called me already. We talk pretty often now."

Olivia groaned. "Now that might be a deal breaker."

CHAPTER THIRTY-EIGHT

"Evie, please stop slurping your soup. I can't stand the noise," Olivia said.

They were enjoying steaming bowls of butternut-squash bisque on Brad and Angie's patio. The sun was setting, casting the clouds in a cotton-candy pink against the light-blue sky. Out here on top of a hill was the perfect vantage point for a mid-autumn sunset.

"I'm trying, but it's so hot."

"Maybe wait for it to cool off?"

"But it's so good." Evie pouted and put her spoon down for a moment.

Brad leaned over with the breadbasket. "Hey, try dipping this bread in it. I know how you feel about this stuff. Ange is an amazing cook."

Evie smiled and took a piece of the sourdough.

"What's it like living with Olivia?" he asked.

"It's good. We're taking boxing lessons together because I punched a kid at school."

"It wasn't nearly hard enough," Olivia said.

Brad laughed, and Angie almost spit out her soup.

"I hope this was in self-defense?" Angie asked.

"Yes. He was harassing me. The principal makes him see the school counselor once a week now."

"She sure does," Olivia said proudly.

Angie elbowed Brad. "When our kiddo comes, we're asking Olivia to be the godparent."

Olivia looked between them and noticed how Brad's face had subtly filled out since she'd seen him last. "Do you have news you'd like to share?"

Brad grabbed Angie's hand. "You'll be the first to know, actually. We found out yesterday that we're having a baby."

"That's great. I'm so happy for you two," she said.

"Thanks. No news yet on how people around here will treat a pregnant man, but I sat down with Aerin's mom at the hospital, and she told me she'd brief the OB/Gyn staff on the whole thing."

"How does it work if you're a man?" Evie asked.

Olivia turned bright red. "It's not polite to ask questions about someone's body," she whispered.

"That's generally true, but I'm happy to talk about it. Basically, Evie, I stopped taking my testosterone so I could get pregnant, and I'll start taking it again once I'm done chest-feeding," Brad said.

"So you still have all your original parts?"

"I have everything I need to carry a child."

"Huh." Evie leaned back in her chair.

"What are you thinking about?" Angie asked.

She shrugged. "Bodies are so cool. I never thought about a man getting pregnant."

"Yeah. If you have any other questions about trans people, you can feel free to ask them. Education is the key to acceptance."

"Director Brad Lowery, everybody," said Angie.

Olivia sheepishly realized she'd never bothered to find out what Brad did for work. "Recent promotion?"

"Actually, Angie and I started a non-profit a few years ago. Indiana Queer Alliance. We call it IQ for All. We do education and outreach to different organizations in the area about how to be more inclusive."

"Whoa. I had no idea," Olivia said. "So, the supermarket job?"

"Just moonlighting for some extra money. It doesn't exactly pay well to run a non-profit."

"Can I volunteer there?" Evie asked.

Brad held up his hand to give her a high five. "Hell, yes. We have tons that you can do."

"Cool."

"We are just about to make some educational videos to post on social media," Angie said.

"You should put me in them. I'm going to go viral."

"Love it. You're hired," Brad said. He pulled his phone from his back pocket and frowned. "Excuse me for a moment."

Olivia watched Brad walk up to the house as he read his phone. When he was done, he gestured in her direction. "Olivia? Can you come here for a second?" She jogged up to the house. "So, we have a bit of a situation."

"We do?" Olivia asked.

"Your mom and Emmanuel. How much did she tell you about how Evie ended up living with you?"

"Enough for me to not want to ask any questions. You knew about this whole thing?"

"Yeah. We do some work with them, mostly to identify kids in need, but sometimes to educate the parents so they can eventually take their kids back."

"Okay, so what's the problem?"

"Your mom was hiding all this from your dad because, well, we all know how he is. Not exactly an upstanding citizen."

"True. She told me a bit about the group she works with. She asked me to help get my brother and her out of the house. I think in another few days or so when Martin finds out."

"He found out today."

"My dad?"

"Yes. He found out and he's livid. She just emailed me that she's not safe there. He took the car keys and her cell phone and set the security system so he'd know if they opened a door or window." Brad's eyes were wide with concern.

Olivia had to lean against a door to steady herself. How could that bastard do this? "We need to get them out of there right now." She thought of her sweet little brother and how scared he must be of being trapped in the house.

"Angie can stay with Evie. I'm going with you," said Brad.

"You sure?"

"Let's get there before he does."

CHAPTER THIRTY-NINE

Brad insisted on driving because his truck seemed like a better getaway vehicle than Olivia's coupe. They arrived at the house in twenty minutes. Martin was nowhere to be found, and Olivia counted her blessings. By now, evening had settled in and the sun had almost set.

"Can you pull around back? Just drive over the grass."

Everyone in town knew that the Ando family kept their yard pristine, just like the inside of the house. Brad hesitated.

"Seriously, just do it."

"This feels so wrong, but here we go." Brad gunned the engine and drove into the backyard. He stopped next to Olivia's childhood swing set.

Just as they turned the corner of the house, Olivia thought she saw headlights coming down the long driveway. "Shit. I think he's here."

"What do we do?"

"You stay in the back so that when he disables the alarm, they can sneak out. I'll distract him." I'll deck him if I have to, she thought. Just two weeks of boxing lessons had given her unearned confidence.

"I'll have my phone, so you can text me when the coast is clear. I'll try to get their attention, if I can figure out which room they're in," Brad said.

Olivia put her fist out and Brad bumped it. "Go, team," she said. The neighborhood was quiet at this time of evening, and Olivia tiptoed around the side of the house. After she heard a car door close around at the front, she took a deep breath and counted to three. She had to catch him right as he went in so the alarm would be off and Mariko could sneak out unseen. Otherwise, there might be a struggle, and she didn't want to actually have to use her boxer training.

Like a practiced burglar, she slithered against the house until she could see the front doorway. Tall hedges obstructed her view of the driveway, and she had to listen carefully to figure out where her father had ended up. She heard the front door open. Heart racing, she sprinted toward the door to get Martin's attention.

"Hey!" she yelled as she ran into the vestibule.

Olivia wasn't prepared to hear a high-pitched scream from someone decidedly more feminine than her father.

"Aerin?"

"Jesus Christ, Olivia. What the fuck?"

"What are you doing here?"

Aerin clutched at her chest, still reeling from the fright. "I'm helping spring your mom and brother. Same as you, it looks like."

"Fuck. I'm sorry. It's good to see you. How did you do that? Do you know about the alarm?"

"Yeah. I disabled it for a fraction of a second, opened the door, and enabled it again."

Olivia took a deep breath and rested her forehead on Aerin's shoulder. "I'm sorry for scaring you. I thought you were my dad."

"It's okay. Let's get them out before that asshole comes back."

"Yeah. You go find my mom and my brother, and I'll watch out for my dad coming home. Brad is in his truck out back. I'll text you if I see Martin, okay?"

She typed out a quick text to Brad to let him know what was going on. When she looked back up, her blood ran ice cold. There was her father, flesh and blood, in front of her. He must have parked down the driveway and walked. Martin seemed as surprised as she was. He'd aged badly in the last decade and a half, probably because of all the hate he was spewing. His face was gaunt and his scalp ringed by gray hairs.

"Olivia?"

She kept staring, unable to propel herself out of the moment, until Martin flinched. It broke the spell, and Olivia stood tall before him. When she hit puberty, she'd surged to almost his height. Now she seemed to tower over him. Perhaps it was the physical dimensions, but Olivia knew it also had to do with power. His was waning as hers grew stronger.

"Leave," she said.

"You shouldn't be here."

Olivia's jaw tightened. "Walk away, and we won't call the police."

To her astonishment, Martin laughed, a strung-out sound that showed he hadn't changed at all in fifteen years. Bastard. "What would the police do? Arrest me for trying to walk into my own house?"

"Arrest you for assaulting your wife and attempting to trap her in her house. I'm sure your congregation would love to hear that. Oh, and also condoning hateful behavior toward one of your young parishioners. Should I go on?"

"They'll never believe you." He stepped closer.

Olivia heard shuffling sounds from upstairs and hoped Aerin sensed Martin's presence. Go out the back, she thought, trying hard to send her message over the space between them. A moment later, a feeling she could only describe as confirmation filled her chest. Had her attempt at telepathy actually worked?

Aerin, Mariko, and Emmanuel obviously were tiptoeing down the back stairs, which were unfortunately made of squeaky old wood. Martin's ears perked up, and he tried to push past Olivia. She used her body to stop him, pushing him back a little. Though she was as tall as he, she wasn't nearly as muscular, and with a heavy shove, she fell backward against the wall. She struggled to her feet, but it was too late. Martin was on his way to the back entrance.

• 203 •

Olivia stumbled after him. He'd blocked the bottom of the stairs. She could hear his disgusting mouth-breathing as he stared at his family and Aerin. Olivia heard Aerin tell Emmanuel to go around the front and get into her car. Olivia waited between the stairways until her little brother ran out the front door, then sprang into action. She needed to distract Martin, or at least knock him off balance long enough for Aerin and Mariko to escape. With two getaway cars, the odds were in their favor.

She ran full speed and slammed into Martin from the side, knocking him against the kitchen counter. The blow stunned him, and he clutched at his ribs in obvious pain. Olivia immediately turned her attention to Aerin and Mariko, who were hustling down the stairs and out the door. They'd done it. Olivia was about to follow them when Martin grabbed the back of her shirt.

"You piece of shit," he said.

Olivia struggled to get free, but Martin was too strong, and he was pulling the shirt too tight for her to wriggle out of it.

"What are you going to do to me? Kill me? Hurt me? Doesn't seem very Christian, does it?" Olivia asked.

"Colossians 3:18: 'Wives, submit yourselves unto your own husbands, as it is fit in the Lord.' Deuteronomy 22:5: 'The woman shall not wear that which pertaineth unto a man, neither shall a man put on a woman's garment: for all that do so are abomination unto the Lord thy God.'"

"Oh, for fuck's sake. You're conveniently forgetting all the ways Jesus asks us to love each other. Want to quote some of those instead?"

Martin scowled. "The Bible says I'm in charge of my family, and I'll do as I see fit. If my wife is out of line, I'm allowed to punish her. Same with my abomination of a daughter."

"Fuck off," Olivia said. She tried not to betray her fear of him, though pretending a two-hundred-pound man was harmless took a lot of effort.

"Get upstairs." He pushed Olivia toward the back stairwell.

"Don't quit your day job, Pastor Ando," someone said behind them. Olivia turned to see Brad filming them with his phone.

"Who the hell are you?"

"Probably your worst nightmare. Actually, I was kidding. Do quit your day job. After this goes viral, you won't have a choice. Let her go, and I'll let you delete this video."

Martin tightened his grip on Olivia and looked between them. After a moment, he reached for Brad's phone, inadvertently loosening his hold on her shirt. Brad handed it to him, and while Martin tried to figure out how to stop filming, Brad picked up a barstool and brought it down over his head. Martin crumpled like a tin can. Brad took his phone, and Olivia ushered him out of there.

"Holy shit, that was awesome. You still have that video, right?"

"Oh, yeah. That was on Instagram Live on the IQ For All page," Brad said. Olivia high-fived him when they got to the truck. "You okay, though?"

"I'm fine. Don't worry about me." She swung herself up to the passenger's seat. Mariko sat in the middle, a shadow of her usual measured self, chewing her fingernails and gazing anxiously out of the truck in all directions.

"Emmanuel is fine. He's in Aerin's car," Olivia said to her mom. "Martin is temporarily disabled. I'll call Aerin."

She picked up on the first ring. "Did you get out of there okay?" Aerin asked.

"Little snag, but we're all fine now. Are you on the road?"

"Heading to your place, if that's okay."

"Of course. We'll meet you there."

After a tense ride to Brad's to pick up Evie, the three of them said good-bye to their friends and left in Olivia's car. Mariko did her best to explain to Evie what had happened, which ended in both of them crying. A feeling of dread permeated the car all the way home. Olivia was sure Martin had been knocked out, but she kept checking the rearview mirror for headlights anyway.

Aerin had let herself in by the time Olivia pulled onto her quiet street. She and Emmanuel stood at the open door, stances low and ready, guarding the house against intruders. Olivia was so relieved to see her there, she almost burst into tears. Every second of their nerve-wracking escape from her father seemed to melt away in Aerin's presence.

Olivia made hot chocolate for the gang, and they sipped it while sitting in the dimly lit living room. Mariko insisted Martin didn't know where his daughter lived, but that was little comfort. Olivia figured he could find out pretty easily. Marsha settled in Evie's lap while Evie leaned into Emmanuel's shoulder. Aerin comforted Mariko, leaving Olivia by herself.

"He grabbed me after you and Mom left," Olivia said.

Aerin looked at her with concern but didn't make a move away from Mariko. "I'm so sorry. Are you okay?"

"Brad hit him over the head with a stool." She chuckled.

"Good thing, too. Martin wasn't going to let you go that easily. Brad got it all on video for the Instagram," Mariko said.

Evie perked up. "I already liked it and shared it with all my Insta friends. I still have some who go to the church. I bet they're sharing it with their parents."

"He's a goner," Emmanuel said, sounding sad.

Olivia realized that despite Martin's abhorrent behavior, Emmanuel still loved him in some way. "It's going to be okay," she said to him, though she didn't quite know how.

"Mom just texted," Aerin said. "They took Martin into the ER. He's handcuffed to the hospital bed." She took a deep breath and blew it out. "I should probably get going. Long day ahead of me tomorrow."

Olivia stood to walk her out. They paused on the top of the steps, Olivia's heart pounding, wanting so badly to ask Aerin to stay with her.

"Well, even though you scared the shit out of me, I'm glad we could get them out."

"Yeah. Thanks for your help," Olivia stammered.

Aerin enveloped her in a tight hug. Olivia loved the way her arms fit around Aerin's back. Aerin's hair caught the wind and blew into Olivia's nose. She breathed in the smell of skin and sweat, wanting to stay forever in their little cocoon. They embraced for a long time, neither willing to let go. When Aerin finally did, she wiped her nose on the back of her hand. Olivia saw the glint of tears on her cheeks as she turned to go.

"Do you have to leave?"

"I should, shouldn't I?"

Olivia shook her head. "I don't know. It doesn't feel right after what happened."

"Where would I sleep?"

"We're a little short on space, but maybe my bed? We can sleep head to toe if you want. I feel safer with you here, even if my dad is in custody."

Aerin looked at her car and then back at Olivia. "Okay."

"Okay?"

Aerin stepped close to Olivia and kissed her briefly. "Okay."

CHAPTER FORTY

A erin leaned against the workbench Cassie had installed in the spare room. Her entire apartment now permanently smelled of sharp metal dust. She was certain she'd lose most of her security deposit based on the dents in the floor, but that was a problem for another day. Right now, she had to figure out whether it was a good idea to continue building the machine.

The notes and accounts from Max didn't help her decision much. Sure, Murray mentioned that he'd regret some future decision of his, but that could be anything at all. Perhaps it was writing down plans for the machine, but more likely, Aerin figured, he regretted going to the lake for the second time. After all, he'd drowned. No one could have a bigger regret than dying. She wished Murray had visited her dreams like he had Olivia's. Starting a fire to unearth these papers was an extremely roundabout way to send her information.

She picked up a bolt that had rolled into a corner and tossed it at the machine. It bounced off with a satisfying clunk and rolled into another corner. The last time she'd tried to make sense of a message, she'd used music, which seemed to unlock an ability to travel to other worlds. Maybe she could use it to contact Murray's ghost or the alien energy that lived inside him. After all, she'd learned in middle school that energy couldn't be destroyed. It could only change form.

Aerin closed her eyes and tried to concentrate on imagining what form Murray might be in. She coaxed her thoughts outward and asked for a response from somewhere. Nothing happened. She sighed and looked down. As she did, her heart began to pound. The bolt she'd thrown was back in its original corner. She picked it up and turned it over with her fingers, studying the grooves in the metal. They spiraled into themselves and then back out. Aerin jumped to her knees. Of course. Murray wasn't gone. He was just trapped in a never-ending spiral somewhere out there. Maybe he wasn't in this dimension or this time, but he was in one of them. If Aerin could figure out how to reach him, she could determine what kind of message he was trying to send her.

She spent the next hour pacing her apartment, coming up with plan after plan for contacting Murray. First, she concentrated hard on the bolt, squeezing it in her palm as she pictured Murray before her. Nothing happened other than the hardware making a painful imprint in her skin. She tried chanting his name like a mantra. Finally, she gave up and tossed the bolt back into the spare room. It was no use.

Aerin needed a glass of water. All that concentrating had made her thirsty. She noticed the time on her microwave clock and panicked. Olivia was due to come over in a few minutes, and Aerin wasn't presentable at all. She was still wearing her pajamas, and her armpits reeked of stress sweat. Praying Olivia would be late, she quickly stripped and jumped into the shower. As she lathered herself up, she had a vision of Olivia in the shower with her, caressing her skin. That's when she heard the buzzer.

Fuck. She wanted Olivia to walk into her apartment right now and find her here in this compromising position. Why had she sold the house and rented an apartment with double security again? To her amazement, a few moments later, she heard her apartment door open and shut.

"Hello?"

"I'm in here," Aerin shouted. She rinsed off and threw one towel around her hair and one around her body. "How'd you get in?"

Olivia popped her head into the bathroom and gave Aerin a quizzical look. "You opened the door for me, and then this one was unlocked?"

"I didn't, though."

"Yeah. You buzzed me up."

Aerin's eyes went wide. She was elated. Maybe the secret to using her powers was not trying? Maybe it was wanting it just enough? It didn't matter either way. Olivia was in her apartment now and looking at her like she was a tall soft-serve ice cream on a hot day.

"I know we were going to go out, but…"

"Same page," Olivia said as she closed the space between them.

They moved from the living-room couch to the bedroom with the practiced ease of two people who knew each other's body. Aerin found it impossible not to feel Olivia's every thought as their skin slid together. Aerin drew out Olivia's orgasm for so long she thought Olivia might actually scream at her. And when it was her turn, Olivia seemed to have the same familiarity with Aerin's desires. With Olivia on top of her, she closed her eyes and felt herself descending into the oblivion of imminent orgasm. And then the strangest thing happened.

Aerin was no longer in bed, moaning against Olivia's shoulder. In front of her stood a computer with lines of code filling the screen. She picked up her hands and gasped. They weren't hers at all. They belonged to a much larger person with skin far darker than hers. She caught a slight reflection in the glass monitor and almost screamed as Stanton's face stared back at her.

"You've figured it out," said a voice deep within her. It was him. She was in his body, aware of his every sensation: the low chuckle emanated from his gut and his amusement at her predicament.

"How the hell did I get here?"

"We're connected, you and I. Part of us is the same being."

"Please tell me you're not in my head right now," she thought.

"I have no use for corporeal pleasures." So he knew what she was up to. Gross.

"I need to get in touch with Murray."

"Then you'll have to make this happen with him." The voice seemed to fade at the end, and suddenly Aerin was back in her bedroom riding the most intense orgasm of her life.

"Whoa," Olivia said as she rolled onto her side. "That was unreal."

"I think I blacked out or something."

"Not based on the sounds you were making." Olivia grinned and kissed her. The kiss became foreplay for another round, and soon Olivia was between her legs. This time she concentrated as hard as she could on Olivia's tongue. She came two more times without body-hopping.

Another check in the "build machine" column: she didn't think anyone else should have to miss an orgasm that fantastic.

CHAPTER FORTY-ONE

The park was almost empty as Olivia set out the picnic blanket. A stroke of luck had brought to the Midwest a gorgeous late-fall day that wasn't overcast, cold, or rainy. She squeezed Aerin's arm, admiring how cute she looked in her new blue puffy vest.

"I'm so glad it's finally done," Aerin said.

Olivia took the small food containers out of her bag and set them on the blanket. "I'm happy for you. Just have to figure out how to use it, and you can have your guest room back. I know Evie wants to sleep somewhere other than the couch."

"I know. Don't guilt me. It'll be over soon. It's the only way to keep the world safe from what's inside me." Aerin sat and leaned back on her elbows. "Give me some of that wine. I need it."

Olivia popped the cork and handed Aerin the bottle. "You sure Cassie doesn't need it more?"

"Cassie definitely needs it more, but they like beer, so I have a fancy case on order at the liquor store."

"You're sweet."

"I couldn't have done it without them. By the way, once this whole thing has passed, I think we should all hang out. You, me, Cassie, Angie, Brad. All the Indiana queers we know."

Olivia chuckled. "Have to include Evie and Tameka then. I hear they're officially going out."

"Let's have one big gay party and invite everyone." She sighed, and her face hardened. "Do you think I'm doing the right thing?"

Olivia had been practicing keeping her opinions to herself in order to support Aerin. After all, Aerin should know best. She was living with the thing they were trying to stop. "I trust you and whatever you decide to do."

"But I don't know anymore. The closer the machine was to being done, the more dread I felt. Now I just can't see that having it is a good idea, but at this point, it's kind of too late."

On the outside, Olivia knew she seemed calm and serene. Inside, she was panicking. Her gut twisted in knots and her palms began to sweat. She thought Aerin knew what she was doing. That's why she'd supported her this whole time. How could she be even less sure now than she had been? "You can always take it apart. We're supposed to be celebrating that it's done, though. We can think of the rest later." She took a deep breath to slow her pounding heart.

"I guess."

"Come on. Whether it's a good idea isn't relevant right now. You built an alien machine from sketches that Murray drew decades ago. That's an engineering feat." What else could she say? *You did a horrible thing. Now go take it apart before anything happens?*

"Technically, Cassie did most of the work."

"Technically, there would have been no work if you hadn't planned it all. Take the win, Aerin." She leaned over and kissed Aerin on the forehead, hoping the sheen of sweat on her upper lip wasn't noticeable. "Let's at least eat this food before it gets even colder, and then we can figure out what to do."

"Okay. Thank you for planning this for me. It feels like our first date."

"We haven't done much actual dating, have we? We should get on that. It's easier now that you have your own place. We don't have to fall into the routine of just sleeping together every two seconds. Not that it was a bad routine."

Aerin nodded. "I'm actually kind of glad we broke up for a while. This seems like a fresh start."

"I still feel like such an asshole for what I said to you."

"Don't. We both needed it. Maybe we could have figured that out before we had a fight in a room filled with floating body parts, but it had to happen."

"I think the body parts added something special. A touch of mortality."

Aerin shook her head and laughed. "Speaking of mortality, I may die if we don't eat soon. I'm starving."

They ate the salads and cookies Olivia had picked up from a local health-food store, then lay back and watched the clouds for a while.

"I'm going to submit that grant next week," said Olivia.

"The one for your new research project?"

"Yeah. I think I have a good chance of getting their attention."

Aerin turned to her and smiled. "I'd say so. Lots of people want to read minds. You just have to figure out how that would work for people who aren't part alien."

"I have some ideas."

Just then, thunder rumbled in the distance.

"Was it supposed to rain today?" Aerin asked. She took out her phone and opened a weather app.

"I didn't think so. There aren't any rain clouds." A flash drew Olivia's attention to a distant pocket of sky. "Did you see that?"

"See what?"

The sky flashed again, and Olivia froze. Red lightning.

"You okay?" Aerin asked.

Olivia started to shake her head and was interrupted by a squirrel running toward the blanket. It looked right at her as it settled on the corner. "Go away, little guy," she said.

"Watch out. It might be rabid. This isn't normal behavior." Aerin stood up and grabbed Olivia, pulling them both away from the advancing rodent.

The squirrel continued to follow them all the way back to the car. "Is it possible he wants something?" Olivia knelt on the ground, ready to be mauled.

The squirrel walked right up to her and hopped onto her sleeve, climbing her like a tree. She giggled at the tiny feet wrapping themselves in her shirt and then on her neck. Far from attacking her, the squirrel settled on her head and cleaned its face.

"What in the world is going on?" Aerin asked warily from the other side of the car.

"I don't know. This squirrel likes me."

"Ugh. That's disgusting. I'm never kissing you again."

"Aw, come on. Look how cute."

"Mr. Piddles would love a squirrel to play with."

Olivia shot Aerin an icy glare and then returned to the small animal on her head. "What are you doing up there, sweetie?"

The squirrel dug its nails into her scalp.

"Ow! What the—"

Destroy the machine. The thought invaded her mind until it was the only thing she could understand. *Destroy it.*

Before she could push the squirrel off her head, it scampered away and ran up a nearby tree. Olivia touched her throbbing scalp, relieved to find her skin intact. Aerin rushed to her side and checked her body for cuts.

"Little bastard. Are you okay?"

Olivia's lip quivered, and she took deep breaths to calm herself. "It spoke to me. It told me to destroy the machine."

"Oh, for fuck's sake. Was it Murray? Couldn't he have been a little clearer in the first place?"

"I don't know who it was, but that squirrel is adamantly anti-machine. Can we go home? I just want to take a shower."

Aerin nodded and grabbed the car keys. "I guess we're not quite as close to the end as we thought."

"What are you going to do?"

"I now have more tallies in the 'destroy-machine' column, so I guess that's what I'll do."

"Yeah, after I recover from being sneak-attacked by a squirrel, I'm happy to help smash that piece of crap."

Aerin and Olivia meant to go back to the apartment as soon as Olivia got out of the shower, but Mariko stalled them in conversation. They didn't make it back to Aerin's apartment until dark.

"Do you think we should smash it?" Olivia asked.

Aerin turned her key in the main door. "Maybe. Or just disassemble it."

"And then smash the parts?" Olivia asked. Aerin raised her eyebrows. "Look, we don't want anyone to be able to put it back together, right? It's like a hard drive."

They passed one of Aerin's neighbors on the stairs and nodded to her, waiting until she was out of sight to resume talking. "I think we also have to get rid of all the papers because someone else could easily build it," Aerin said. She didn't say who she thought might be interested in doing that. Olivia was probably thinking the same.

At her apartment door, Aerin began to feel wary, like something was off. She stopped for a moment to figure out what it was, then laughed at herself when she realized it was just her wreath. It had been knocked a few inches to one side. Almost anything could have done that. It could have been a child running through, delivery people. When she opened the door, though, she dropped her keys onto the floor.

Olivia jumped at the crash. "What's wrong?" She must have seen it then because her eyes became as wide as Aerin's felt.

"Uh, what do we do?" Aerin asked. Her pulse pounded in her throat. Panic set in as she stared into the spare room. The machine was gone.

"Oh, shit. Who do you think took it?"

They looked at each other. Besides Aerin, only one person had a use for the finished machine.

"Fucking Stanton. I can't believe his fucking gall." Olivia fumed. She paced around the apartment, Aerin too shocked to move at all. "Unbelievable. Just when you think it can't possibly get worse."

"I built it so that once it's activated, the portal should close rather than open."

"And you think Stanton doesn't know that and can't figure out how to reverse that one crucial piece you told me about? All you have to do is turn it around, right?"

Aerin sighed and put her head in her hands. "You're right. We have to stop him. We have no choice."

Olivia stopped her pacing to put an arm around Aerin. "I really have no interest in ever going back to that place."

"Neither do I." Aerin shrugged. "But we have to."

"Yeah. He has to be on the road, right? You can't take something like that on a plane."

"Unless he got a private plane. You know he can convince anyone of anything."

"Fly or drive?"

Aerin walked over to the couch and flopped onto its luxurious white cushions. "I just want to take a nap."

"Flying it is. I'll get us on the next plane, and you bring some clothes for us. Call my mom, too. She and the kids will be fine without me for a few days."

"Okay, okay. I'm getting up in a minute." Aerin had no actual intention of getting up ever, until she remembered she had a world to save.

They were on the road to the airport in record time and at the Rochester Airport a few hours after that. Aerin would have said everything was going according to plan, except that she had none.

She had no idea where they might find Stanton and, once they did, what they could do. He was far more powerful than either of them, as she'd experienced firsthand, and he could have been planning this for years. That left them only one choice: they had to surprise and outsmart him. But how did you outsmart an all-seeing alien-human hybrid with only one goal in life? She was at a complete loss.

Olivia argued that the chance Stanton would deploy the machine in the middle of the night was scant, so they checked into a hotel near the airport. They planned to go directly to the lake the next morning. Olivia splurged for a king suite with a hot tub. Even if they didn't have time to use it, Aerin was glad to have the special touch. Tomorrow they'd be facing Goliath, so tonight, small luxuries meant the world.

Aerin curled Olivia around her like a vise as they slept fitfully. The horrors that might await them in the morning became distant nightmares for a while. They woke in the early morning hours, just as the sun was rising. Aerin joined Olivia in the shower, wanting to relish what neither would admit could be their last hours together. They kissed under the spray for so long, Aerin's fingers were pruney by the time they dried off.

"Glad we brought the coats. Looks cold outside," Olivia said. She put on some clothes she'd left at Aerin's apartment and layered one of Aerin's winter jackets on top.

Aerin felt the chill just by looking out the window. A sparkling frost dusted everything outside their cozy hotel room. Winter was well on its way in upstate New York, and Aerin wasn't ready for it.

Olivia cradled her from behind, her arms warm and reassuring. "Ready to go save the world?"

CHAPTER FORTY-THREE

Aerin was numb as the frozen grass outside as they walked to their rental car.

"Hey, at least it's not a goddamn minivan this time, right?" Olivia said. They buckled their seat belts and looked at each other.

"Heh." Aerin appreciated her attempt at humor, but she wasn't in the mood. She wanted this over and done with.

"What are the chances you've figured out how to harness your powers and actually stop Stanton?"

"About zero percent. I've tried and tried, but I've had luck only when I'm not trying. We're screwed."

"Hm. Remember when I saw something flash in the sky yesterday?"

Aerin crossed her arms. "Before the rabid squirrel crawled on your head?"

"I think that somehow I ended up with some kind of powers, too. When I went exploring on Rhuna One during that dream I told you about, I saw this red lightning. When I woke up that morning, I swore that I could see it again for a moment. It was the same thing I spotted yesterday. Yes, after the rabid squirrel." She rolled her eyes.

Aerin let out a sharp breath and leaned back in the seat. "You think it's the alien energy? It can get transferred in ways other than the lake?"

"I'm thinking so. I've been pretty hungry since I had the dream. It would explain a lot. Anyway, I just want you to know that if anything happens, I have your back," Olivia said.

"Thanks." Sure, having a souped-up version of Olivia there was better than actually being alone, but when it came to stopping Stanton, she had her doubts. "Two people who may have but don't know how to use powers. Great. Should be a good match for Stanton."

"And whoever he decides to bring with him this time."

They got to the lake just after nine in the morning. Its pristine waters sloshed against the shoreline in a way that made Aerin question whether she'd dreamt the explosion. How could something so beautiful be the scene of such horror?

"Should we wait in here?" Olivia asked.

Aerin nodded. They could see a huge swath of shoreline. If Stanton showed up, they would spot him. It was toasty in the car with the heat on and almost felt like any other day. She'd have loved this to be a date. She'd make out with Olivia on the waterfront, and maybe they'd go park somewhere and screw in the backseat like teenagers.

"What are you thinking about?" Olivia asked.

"You. Us. How much I want this to be over and also not happening at all." She smiled and felt her expression quickly fade away.

"I'd love to be back in that hotel again with you. It was so nice to sleep like that." Olivia took Aerin's hand and brought it to her lips. "I want a hundred more years of that. I don't want to let you go, ever."

"Maybe we'll be transported somewhere else and live forever in our own little world," Aerin said wistfully.

"I'd give anything for that."

They sat in silence through eight oldies songs, Aerin resting her head on Olivia's shoulder. She'd almost fallen asleep when a knock on their back window made them both jump.

"Jesus, what was that?" Aerin asked.

Olivia narrowed her eyes as she looked into the rearview mirror. "What do you think that was? Come on. Let's go."

Aerin exited the car and walked toward Stanton, who sat on the trunk. He was alone, and the machine sat at his feet. Seeing it for the first time in broad daylight was alarming. The blood rushed to her ears as she confronted the truth of the matter. Stanton had indeed broken in and taken it.

"Thank you for this, Aerin," he said.

"You stole that from me."

"Yes."

Aerin's temper flared at Stanton's calmness. It seemed to be an inverse reaction. "I cannot express the amount that I hate you right now. Why couldn't you build it yourself if you were just going to steal it from me?"

"If I built it myself, would you be here right now?"

Aerin looked at Olivia on the other side of the car and suddenly understood. They shouldn't have come here at all. How could she have been so naive?

Take the machine and run, Aerin thought to Olivia. Go. She tried to give eye signals to match her dire instructions, but it didn't matter. Stanton could hear everything.

"I'm sorry, but you won't be taking this machine anywhere. We have all we need right here, right now."

"Aerin, get in the car," Olivia said. She gestured toward the front seat. Aerin tried to move toward the door, but her feet wouldn't budge. She'd guessed right. Neither of them was powerful enough to handle Stanton.

She wracked her brain for a plan. They needed a different tactic, one that Stanton couldn't anticipate. Aerin thought back to Zoe's house when she'd cornered Stanton, or, rather, he'd cornered her. He said something about the future being set until certain moments, turning points. They had to find one, a moment that would set the future on a path Stanton wasn't expecting. It was the only way he could be surprised, and even then, they had seconds to act at most. He'd quickly be able to anticipate their next move. The problem was, she couldn't see her future anymore. Finding a turning point would be a shot in the dark.

Aerin looked between Olivia and Stanton. "We can't change the future," she said to Olivia. "He can see what's about to happen here. That's been set. But Stanton told me that there are moments beyond that he can't see."

Stanton began to chuckle. "Do you think you'll be able to outsmart me with the knowledge I gave you?"

"Olivia, each of those moments is a choice. If we make one he's not expecting, we can stop him."

Olivia nodded. "I'm with you." She moved back toward Stanton and the machine. He laughed again as he led them down the grass toward the shore.

Aerin could see her breath like a ghost as the three of them walked with the machine. Stanton seemed unworried, humming a little tune to himself as if he didn't have any worries. Maybe he didn't. Aerin had no idea how this would turn out. She felt raw and exhausted, at her most vulnerable, probably where Stanton needed her to be. Right now, she'd give up a limb as a sacrifice to Stanton. Anything to return her life to how it was before.

She soon realized Stanton wanted her to do what she'd done last time at the lake, concentrate her energy on the machine to make it work. Along with his power, the machine would beam a ray of electrons into the lake to open the portal. Murray had written as much, and Stanton had started the process of concentration. Aerin had no choice but to follow. She had one last hope: the funnel's direction, changed by Murray in his drawings and placed in that same direction by Cassie. She glanced just inside the machine to see if Stanton had reversed it. He had. It was set to work as originally intended, to open the portal rather than to close it.

Her mind became less and less available to her as Stanton directed her concentration to the machine. Aerin grasped at any hint of an option for stopping him. Did he know about Olivia, that she'd somehow managed to gain her own powers through a dream? Aerin hadn't seen any evidence of these gifts, but if Olivia said it was true, she'd be the last person to doubt her. If Aerin was correct and Stanton had no idea, Olivia might be their Trojan horse. Perhaps she'd tip the balance just enough to throw Stanton off.

The machine began to whir, electrifying the air around it. Aerin's arm hair stood on end, and she glanced at Olivia, who had a strange, almost terrified, look on her face. Aerin gazed at the space around her and realized why. She was shimmering like a mirage. Her concentration became fully consumed by the whirring of the metal components, and she closed her eyes to listen to the tone. It drew her in as sound had many times before. This was different, though. After this, there would be no more noises.

Aerin jerked her eyes open. No more noise? She saw peace in her future. She saw herself alone in her apartment, drinking tea on the white couch, a photograph of Olivia on her coffee table. Through the rippling air she noticed the machine had grown bigger. No, it wasn't the machine at all. It was Olivia, draped over it like a rag doll.

❖

Olivia watched helplessly as Aerin and Stanton grew bright with energy. Panicking, she ran to the lake and picked a large rock from the bottom. It was cold and wet and numbed her hand as she drew it back. This was her only chance. Stanton didn't appear to be paying attention as she heaved it toward him, but the rock glanced off his aura and fell in the grass. Damn it. She had no idea what to do to make this stop, and Aerin was too far gone to help. She was their only chance.

The machine began to emit a translucent blue beam in the direction of the lake. As Olivia tried to make sense of the new development, the beam grew wider and as tall as a person. All of a sudden, she knew what she had to do. It was laid out in front of her as a clear pathway, a means to an end. A turning point, she thought bitterly as she saw the result in her mind. If this was the sacrifice she had to make to ensure her family had a chance to survive as themselves, she'd gladly make it.

Olivia took one more look at Aerin, luminous and lovely behind her veil of energy, and stepped into the beam.

CHAPTER FORTY-FOUR

The smell of burning metal wafted through the air as Aerin dragged Olivia's body away from the machine. She could see smoke billowing from one of the holes when she looked back. Good. The piece of shit was ruined. Stanton still appeared to be stuck in a trance, and Aerin thanked the heavens for this small miracle.

She laid Olivia on the grass and listened for breath. None came, no pulse. Aerin's visions of her future flooded her mind and she began to understand. What she'd seen was a world without Olivia.

"No," she cried. If Olivia's death was the turning point, she wanted the alternative. She wanted the aliens to come and take over, change the course of humanity, change civilization. Anything to keep her Olivia alive. She wept over Olivia's lifeless body, unable to focus on anything else, even as Stanton grunted in the background.

"This wasn't supposed to happen," he said.

Aerin heard a sizzle and moan of pain, then heavy footsteps walking away. She laid her head on Olivia's still-warm chest and imagined a different reality, one in which they'd both walked away unhurt, gone back home, hugged their families, cried tears of joy rather than anguish, kissed each other every second they could.

To her astonishment, a warmth grew in her chest. She sat up and touched her hand over her heart, felt it radiating with heat. Aerin's chest began to sting as she saw the space between herself and Olivia glow red. The color of Olivia's lightning, she remembered. Olivia the human might be dead, but the alien energy inside her was reaching out, probing into Aerin to borrow some of her life force.

Just as the pain in her core grew so intense that Aerin almost screamed, she heard a gasp.

"Olivia?"

Another heaving breath shook Olivia as she arched from the ground then thumped back down. Then silence. Aerin waited anxiously for something to happen, too terrified to touch Olivia and break whatever magic spell this was. Moments went by without change, and Aerin began to think the breaths Olivia seemed to take were part of her wishful imagination.

She'd almost burst into tears again when she heard a low, rhythmic sound, almost like a pulse, in her ears. She put her hand over her own heart and felt the muscle pump over and over. The heartbeat wasn't hers, though. It was Olivia's.

CHAPTER FORTY-FIVE

Meg brought two steaming bowls down the basement stairs.

"Thanks, Mom," Aerin said.

Olivia stirred from sleep and turned her head toward the side table. "That smells amazing. What is that?" Olivia's words were slurred.

"Your favorite, honey. Oatmeal soup."

"Sounds disgusting, but I'm so hungry."

"Yeah. You have to work on your descriptions a bit, Mom," Aerin said.

"When it's the only food you've eaten for three days, does it really matter?" Meg asked.

Olivia chuckled. "I think I can eat something else now. Can you make me a smoothie?"

Meg squeezed Aerin's shoulder. "Progress."

As Meg took the oatmeal back up to the kitchen, Mariko came down the stairs.

"How is she feeling?" she asked Aerin.

"I'm awake, Mom. Tired, but better," Olivia said.

"How's the burn?"

Aerin lifted the sheet that covered Olivia's hospital bed. "Almost gone."

"A miracle from God. No matter what your father says, God loves you," Mariko said.

Aerin placed the sheet back over Olivia and kissed her cheek. "Someone does."

She took Olivia's hand and felt both their pulses quicken. She could tell Olivia wanted to be alone with her, but it was too soon for sex. They were just beginning to discover the ways they were now connected, and Aerin thought it best to proceed cautiously. She projected calmness into Olivia and felt her desire quell.

"If Stanton is anything to go by, we have at least another century together," Aerin said.

Olivia smiled and squeezed Aerin's hand as she settled back into a nap.

Later that night, as Olivia was sleeping soundly in the basement, Aerin built a small fire outside and threw all of Murray's papers into it. She watched them curl at the edges as the flames consumed them. She stayed well after the fire had burned itself out, hugging a winter parka around herself.

Her phone still had Zoe's text on its lock screen. She read it again. *Stanton's gone.* She'd have welcomed the news at any other moment, but with him still in possession of the machine, it read like a warning. He'd fix it and find some other unsuspecting alien-human hybrid to help him set it off. Until then, though, Aerin could relax in the knowledge that the world was safe tonight and her one true love was alive and hers again.

EPILOGUE

Aerin walked down a long, sterile corridor toward chattering voices. The fluorescent lights along the ceiling flickered from a known instability in the old technology. She looked down at her shoes, sensible and dark brown, topped by a flowing pair of white pants. A bold choice she wouldn't have made in her youth.

Halfway down the hall was the room she would turn into, full of the rest of her team, the Task Force for a New Humanity. She'd advocated for a better acronym, something more like Consciousness of Tomorrow (CoT), or Bringing About Change on Earth (BACE). She'd been outvoted, but she wasn't upset. They had a lot of work left to do, which was more important than what they called themselves.

"Welcome, Aerin," Evie said, standing to give her a hug. She'd grown into a tall, slender woman with a gift for spreading their message.

"Hi, sweetie. Are you eating enough? You're looking thin."

"You know how it is. I haven't integrated yet, but I get so sick of eating when food is just fuel."

"How are your parents?"

"They're good. They're out with Tameka's parents to plan some kind of surprise for the wedding. Anyway, we're ready to start when you are."

Aerin nodded and looked at the group. There were one hundred and sixty-seven of them so far, and most of them were in this room. Absent was Olivia, who was giving a talk that night, and Stanton, whose time had run out several years ago. He'd never repaired the machine. His energy had been passed to a small group of passengers who were on the same bus the night his body died. The passengers were all here.

"Okay, Angie, what's the target today?" Aerin asked.

Angie had left IQ for All in the hands of a capable director a few years ago and had taken the top position in TFNH. "Today we're focusing on a small region in Brazil where water wars have broken out in the last few days. The government is withholding water. In fact, one individual named Roberto Salazar is coordinating the blockade in our region. We should focus on him and his associates. I think we can get them to stand down."

"Thanks. Let's begin," Aerin said. She sat in a chair at the edge of the long chain of seats that curled into itself, forming a giant spiral. Tight quarters were the best way to maintain contact. She grabbed Angie's hand on one side and Evie's on the other and closed her eyes.

Her power alone could easily sway one or two people in her vicinity, but she'd discovered that coordination increased the range of persuasion enough so they could reach anywhere in the world. Together, the group concentrated on Brazil, homing in on Salazar. Aerin felt him right away, terrified of the rioters and bound by loyalty. A dangerous place to be, scared and inflexible. They would change that. Soon he'd be on the side of good, and a seed would be sown so he'd begin to influence those around him. Olivia's work with mind-influencing music had given them the notes they needed to sway Salazar and open his mind to a higher consciousness.

The entire room began to hum the dissonant melody. Aerin spoke to him, whispering the ways in which she wanted him to be better. She felt Salazar's anger slow, then fade away altogether. Once it was gone, Aerin knew his sense of morality would blossom, and he would do the right thing. He would relieve his fellow countrymen of their thirst, and then he would join the rebellion. The answer to ending strife was complicated, plated with layers of historical and institutional injustice. The small difference TFNH made, though, was creating waves.

Once the riot had ended, Aerin broke contact with Evie and Angie. The rest of the room followed, exhausted. One down, a million more to go.

About the Author

Jane C. Esther is a librarian by day and a writer by night. Her idea of a good time involves a microscope, binoculars, trashy TV about the British royal family, or randomly singing Broadway show tunes. You can find her recounting the results of the latest scientific studies to whoever will listen, and secretly transforming her house into an indoor vegetable farm. She lives in New England with her wife and dog, and can be reached at www.janecesther.com.

Books Available from Bold Strokes Books

All the Paths to You by Morgan Lee Miller. High school sweethearts Quinn Hughes and Kennedy Reed reconnect five years after they break up and realize that their chemistry is all but over. (978-1-63555-662-9)

Arrested Pleasures by Nanisi Barrett D'Arnuck. When charged with a crime she didn't commit Katherine Lowe faces the question: Which is harder, going to prison or falling in love? (978-1-63555-684-1)

Bonded Love by Renee Roman. Carpenter Blaze Carter suffers an injury that shatters her dreams, and ER nurse Trinity Greene hopes to show her that sometimes hope is worth fighting for. (978-1-63555-530-1)

Convergence by Jane C. Esther. With life as they know it on the line, can Aerin McLeary and Olivia Ando's love survive an otherworldly threat to humankind? (978-1-63555-488-5)

Coyote Blues by Karen F. Williams. Riley Dawson, psychotherapist and shape-shifter, has her world turned upside down when Fiona Bell, her one true love, returns. (978-1-63555-558-5)

Drawn by Carsen Taite. Will the clues lead Detective Claire Hanlon to the killer terrorizing Dallas, or will she merely lose her heart to person of interest, urban artist Riley Flynn? (978-1-63555-644-5)

Every Summer Day by Lee Patton. Meant to celebrate every summer day, Luke's journal instead chronicles a love affair as fast-moving and possibly as fatal as his brother's brain tumor. (978-1-63555-706-0)

Lucky by Kris Bryant. Was Serena Evans's luck really about winning the lottery, or is she about to get even luckier in love? (978-1-63555-510-3)

The Last Days of Autumn by Donna K. Ford. Autumn and Caroline question the fairness of life, the cruelty of loss, and what it means to love as they navigate the complicated minefield of relationships, grief, and life-altering illness. (978-1-63555-672-8)

Three Alarm Response by Erin Dutton. In the midst of tragedy, can these first responders find love and healing? Three stories of courage, bravery, and passion. (978-1-63555-592-9)

Veterinary Partner by Nancy Wheelton. Callie and Lauren are determined to keep their hearts safe but find that taking a chance on love is the safest option of all. (978-1-63555-666-7)

Everyday People by Louis Barr. When film star Diana Danning hires private eye Clint Steele to find her son, Clint turns to his former West Point barracks mate, and ex-buddy with benefits, Mars Hauser to lend his cyber espionage and digital black ops skills to the case. (978-1-63555-698-8)

Forging a Desire Line by Mary P. Burns. When Charley's ex-wife, Tricia, is diagnosed with inoperable cancer, the private duty nurse Tricia hires turns out to be the handsome and aloof Joanna, who ignites something inside Charley she isn't ready to face. (978-1-63555-665-0)

Love on the Night Shift by Radclyffe. Between ruling the night shift in the ER at the Rivers and raising her teenage daughter, Blaise Richilieu has all the drama she needs in her life, until a dashing young attending appears on the scene and relentlessly pursues her. (978-1-63555-668-1)

Olivia's Awakening by Ronica Black. When the daring and dangerously gorgeous Eve Monroe is hired to get Olivia Savage into shape, a fierce passion ignites, causing both to question everything they've ever known about love. (978-1-63555-613-1)

The Duchess and the Dreamer by Jenny Frame. Clementine Fitzroy has lost her faith and love of life. Can dreamer Evan Fox make her believe in life and dream again? (978-1-63555-601-8)

The Road Home by Erin Zak. Hollywood actress Gwendolyn Carter is about to discover that losing someone you love sometimes means gaining someone to fall for. (978-1-63555-633-9)

Waiting for You by Elle Spencer. When passionate past-life lovers meet again in the present day, one remembers it vividly and the other isn't so sure. (978-1-63555-635-3)

While My Heart Beats by Erin McKenzie. Can a love born amidst the horrors of the Great War survive? (978-1-63555-589-9)

Face the Music by Ali Vali. Sweet music is the last thing that happens when Nashville music producer Mason Liner, and daughter of country royalty Victoria Roddy are thrown together in an effort to save country star Sophie Roddy's career. (978-1-63555-532-5)

Flavor of the Month by Georgia Beers. What happens when baker Charlie and chef Emma realize their differing paths have led them right back to each other? (978-1-63555-616-2)

Mending Fences by Angie Williams. Rancher Bobbie Del Rey and veterinarian Grace Hammond are about to discover if heartbreaks of the past can ever truly be mended. (978-1-63555-708-4)

Silk and Leather: Lesbian Erotica with an Edge edited by Victoria Villasenor. This collection of stories by award winning authors offers fantasies as soft as silk and tough as leather. The only question is: How far will you go to make your deepest desires come true? (978-1-63555-587-5)

The Last Place You Look by Aurora Rey. Dumped by her wife and looking for anything but love, Julia Pierce retreats to her hometown, only to rediscover high school friend Taylor Winslow, who's secretly crushed on her for years. (978-1-63555-574-5)

The Mortician's Daughter by Nan Higgins. A singer on the verge of stardom discovers she must give up her dreams to live a life in service to ghosts. (978-1-63555-594-3)

The Real Thing by Laney Webber. When passion flares between actress Virginia Green and masseuse Allison McDonald, can they be sure it's the real thing? (978-1-63555-478-6)

What the Heart Remembers Most by M. Ullrich. For college sweethearts Jax Levine and Gretchen Mills, could an accident be the second chance neither knew they wanted? (978-1-63555-401-4)

White Horse Point by Andrews & Austin. Mystery writer Taylor James finds herself falling for the mysterious woman on White Horse Point who lives alone, protecting a secret she can't share about a murderer who walks among them. (978-1-63555-695-7)

Femme Tales by Anne Shade. Six women find themselves in their own real-life fairy tales when true love finds them in the most unexpected ways. (978-1-63555-657-5)

Jellicle Girl by Stevie Mikayne. One dark summer night, Beth and Jackie go out to the canoe dock. Two years later, Beth is still carrying the weight of what happened to Jackie. (978-1-63555-691-9)

Le Berceau by Julius Eks. If only Ben could tear his heart in two, then he wouldn't have to choose between the love of his life and the most beautiful boy he has ever seen. (978-1-63555-688-9)

My Date with a Wendigo by Genevieve McCluer. Elizabeth Rosseau finds her long lost love and the secret community of fiends she's now a part of. (978-1-63555-679-7)

On the Run by Charlotte Greene. Even when they're cute blondes, it's stupid to pick up hitchhikers, especially when they've just broken out of prison, but doing so is about to change Gwen's life forever. (978-1-63555-682-7)

Perfect Timing by Dena Blake. The choice between love and family has never been so difficult, and Lynn's and Maggie's different visions of the future may end their romance before it's begun. (978-1-63555-466-3)

The Mail Order Bride by R Kent. When a mail order bride is thrust on Austin, he must choose between the bride he never wanted or the dream he lives for. (978-1-63555-678-0)

Through Love's Eyes by C.A. Popovich. When fate reunites Brittany Yardin and Amy Jansons, can they move beyond the pain of their past to find love? (978-1-63555-629-2)

To the Moon and Back by Melissa Brayden. Film actress Carly Daniel thinks that stage work is boring and unexciting, but when she accepts a lead role in a new play, stage manager Lauren Prescott tests both her heart and her ability to share the limelight. (978-1-63555-618-6)

Tokyo Love by Diana Jean. When Kathleen Schmitt is given the opportunity to be on the cutting edge of AI technology, she never thought a failed robotic love companion would bring her closer to her neighbor, Yuriko Velucci, and finding love in unexpected places. (978-1-63555-681-0)

Brooklyn Summer by Maggie Cummings. When opposites attract, can a summer of passion and adventure lead to a lifetime of love? (978-1-63555-578-3)

City Kitty and Country Mouse by Alyssa Linn Palmer. Pulled in two different directions, can a city kitty and country mouse fall in love and make it work? (978-1-63555-553-0)

Elimination by Jackie D. When a dangerous homegrown terrorist seeks refuge with the Russian mafia, the team will be put to the ultimate test. (978-1-63555-570-7)

In the Shadow of Darkness by Nicole Stiling. Angeline Vallencourt is a reluctant vampire who must decide what she wants more—obscurity, revenge, or the woman who makes her feel alive. (978-1-63555-624-7)

On Second Thought by C. Spencer. Madisen is falling hard for Rae. Even single life and co-parenting are beginning to click. At least, that is, until her ex-wife begins to have second thoughts. (978-1-63555-415-1)

Out of Practice by Carsen Taite. When attorney Abby Keane discovers the wedding blogger tormenting her client is the woman she had a passionate, anonymous vacation fling with, sparks and subpoenas fly. Legal Affairs: one law firm, three best friends, three chances to fall in love. (978-1-63555-359-8)

Providence by Leigh Hays. With every click of the shutter, photographer Rebekiah Kearns finds it harder and harder to keep Lindsey Blackwell in focus without getting too close. (978-1-63555-620-9)

Taking a Shot at Love by KC Richardson. When academic and athletic worlds collide, will English professor Celeste Bouchard and basketball coach Lisa Tobias ignore their attraction to achieve their professional goals? (978-1-63555-549-3)

CPSIA information can be obtained
at www.ICGtesting.com
Printed in the USA
LVHW111149071222
734753LV00004B/82